TRIPS IN TIME

NINE STORIES OF SCIENCE FICTION

EDITED BY ROBERT SILVERBERG

publishers since 1798

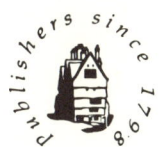

THOMAS NELSON INC., PUBLISHERS
Nashville New York

No character in this book is intended to represent any actual person; all the incidents of the stories are entirely fictional in nature.

Copyright © 1977 by Robert Silverberg

All rights reserved under International and Pan-American Conventions. Published in Nashville, Tennessee, by Thomas Nelson Inc., Publishers, and simultaneously in Don Mills, Ontario, by Thomas Nelson & Sons (Canada) Limited. Manufactured in the United States of America.

First edition

Library of Congress Cataloging in Publication Data
Main entry under title:

Trips in time.

CONTENTS: Priest, C. An infinite summer.—Sheckley, R. The King's wishes.—Phillips, P. Manna. [etc.]
1. Science fiction, American. 2. Science fiction, English. I. Silverberg, Robert.
PZ1.T743 [PS648.S3]   813'.0876   77-24213
ISBN 0-8407-6574-6

ACKNOWLEDGMENTS

An Infinite Summer, by Christopher Priest. Copyright © 1976 by Futura Publications, Ltd. Reprinted by permission of the author.
The King's Wishes, by Robert Sheckley. Copyright 1953 by Fantasy House, Inc. Reprinted by permission of the author and his agent, Sterling Lord.
Manna, by Peter Phillips. Copyright 1949 by Street & Smith Publications, Inc. Reprinted by permission of the author and his agents, Scott Meredith Literary Agency, Inc.
The Long Remembering, by Poul Anderson. Copyright © 1957 by Mercury Press, Inc. Reprinted by permission of the author and his agents, Scott Meredith Literary Agency, Inc.
Try and Change the Past, by Fritz Leiber. Copyright © 1958 by Street & Smith Publications, Inc. Reprinted by permission of the author and his agents, Robert P. Mills, Ltd.
Divine Madness, by Roger Zelazny. Copyright © 1966 by Health Knowledge, Inc. Reprinted by permission of the author and his agents, Henry Morrison, Inc.
MUgwump 4, by Robert Silverberg. Copyright © 1959 by Galaxy Publishing Corp., Inc. Reprinted by permission of the author and his agents, Scott Meredith Literary Agency, Inc.
Secret Rider, by Marta Randall. Copyright © 1976 by Marta Randall. Reprinted by permission of the author.
The Seesaw, by A. E. van Vogt. Copyright 1941 by Street & Smith Publications, Inc. Reprinted by permission of the author and his agent, Forrest J. Ackerman.

TRIPS IN TIME

BOOKS BY ROBERT SILVERBERG

The Masks of Time
The Time Hoppers
Hawksbill Station
To Live Again
Recalled to Life
Starman's Quest
Tower of Glass
Earthmen and Strangers (*editor*)
Voyagers in Time (*editor*)
Men and Machines (*editor*)
Tomorrow's Worlds (*editor*)
Revolt on Alpha C
Lost Race of Mars
Time of the Great Freeze
Conquerors from the Darkness
Planet of Death
The Gate of Worlds
The Calibrated Alligator
Needle in a Timestack
To Open the Sky
Thorns
Worlds of Maybe (*editor*)
Mind to Mind (*editor*)
The Science Fiction Bestiary (*editor*)
The Day the Sun Stood Still (*compiler*)
Beyond Control (*editor*)
Chains of the Sea (*compiler*)
Deep Space (*editor*)
Sundance and Other Science Fiction Stories
Mutants: Eleven Stories of Science Fiction (*editor*)
Threads of Time (*compiler*)
Sunrise on Mercury and Other Science Fiction Stories
Explorers of Space: Eight Stories of Science Fiction (*editor*)
Strange Gifts: Eight Stories of Science Fiction (*editor*)
The Aliens: Seven Stories of Science Fiction (*editor*)
The Crystal Ship: Three Original Novellas of Science Fiction (*editor*)
Earth Is the Strangest Planet: Ten Stories of Science Fiction (*editor*)

CONTENTS

Introduction		9
An Infinite Summer	Christopher Priest	11
The King's Wishes	Robert Sheckley	36
Manna	Peter Phillips	48
The Long Remembering	Poul Anderson	78
Try and Change the Past	Fritz Leiber	93
Divine Madness	Roger Zelazny	102
MUgwump 4	Robert Silverberg	110
Secret Rider	Marta Randall	132
The Seesaw	A. E. van Vogt	160

TRIPS IN TIME

INTRODUCTION

The only workable time machine ever invented is the science-fiction story. No other mechanism yet devised has the same efficient capacity to transport subjects to the distant reaches of the space-time continuum, effortlessly and without significant expenditure of energy . . . and even to bring them back.

Of all the basic themes of science fiction, I think that of voyaging in time is the most fundamental, the closest to the heart of the matter. Stories of spaceships journeying toward distant suns, of flawless robots transforming human civilization, of mutants with strange mental or physical powers are all very fine so far as they go; but they are only *aspects* of the essential science-fiction thing, which for me is to reveal the future. That was what drew me to science fiction myself, when I was eight or nine years old: frustrated by my awareness that I would never live to see the world of the twenty-second century, let alone the world of the thousandth millennium, I turned to H. G. Wells and Robert Heinlein and Jack Williamson and A. E. van Vogt, because they could give me dazzling glimpses of how it *might* be, and I knew that that was the best I could hope for. Science fiction became my time machine. And the stories of robots and spaceships and mutants and all the rest of the classic concepts provided various fragments of the future—but the stories of travel in time gave me the future itself, the fundamental thing, the unattainable world to come. As a reader and then as a writer I was drawn constantly to that.

The present anthology contains relatively few time-machine stories. For one thing, I have already assembled a collection of my favorites of that sort (*Voyagers in Time*, 1967); for another, I want to offer here a group of time-travel stories of a different sort, more subtle variants on the basic notion, stories of people who float back and forth along the time stream in ways even more intricate than those imagined by the old pioneer, H. G. Wells. I think they succeed in providing that heady sense of liberation from the rigid three-dimensional confines of reality that science fiction so uniquely affords. And they provide, also, that sense of strangeness, that sense of peering into unfathomable deeps, which keeps us returning to science fiction again and again.

—Robert Silverberg

AN INFINITE SUMMER
CHRISTOPHER PRIEST

Christopher Priest is a young British writer whose work has been appearing in print since the mid-1960's with steadily increasing impact. His novels, Inverted World, Indoctrinaire, *and* The Space Machine, *have attracted critical acclaim and a wide readership, and his short stories have been published in the leading magazines and anthologies. The strange, sensitive, and eloquent tale reprinted here has never before been published in the United States, but I think we will be encountering it again and again, for not only is it an ingenious piece of science fiction, but it evokes the pain of lost love, of the separations time imposes, in a striking and poignant fashion.*

August, 1940
There was a war on, but it made no difference to Thomas James Lloyd. The war was an inconvenience, and it restricted his freedom, but on the whole it was the least of his preoccupations. Misfortune had brought him to this violent age, and he wanted none of its crises. He was apart from it, shadowed by it.

He stood now on the bridge over the Thames at Richmond, resting his hands on the parapet and staring south along the river. The sun reflected up from it, and he took his sunglasses from a metal case in his pocket and put them on.

Night was the only relief from the tableaux of frozen time; dark glasses approximated the relief.

It seemed to Thomas Lloyd that it was not long since he had last stood untroubled on this bridge, although by deduction he knew that this was not so. The memory of the day was clear, itself a moment of frozen time, undiminished. He remembered how he had stood here with his cousin, watching four young men from the town as they manhandled a punt upstream.

Richmond itself had changed from that time, but here by the river the view was much as he remembered it. Although there were more buildings along the banks, the meadows below Richmond Hill were untouched, and he could see the riverside walk disappearing around the bend in the river towards Twickenham.

For the moment the town was quiet. An air-raid alert had been sounded a few minutes before, and although there were still some vehicles moving through the streets, most pedestrians had taken temporary shelter inside shops and offices.

Lloyd had left them to walk again through the past.

He was a tall, well-built man, apparently young in years. He had been taken for twenty-five several times by strangers and Lloyd, a withdrawn, uncommunicative man, had allowed such errors to go uncorrected. Behind the dark glasses his eyes were still bright with the hopes of youth, but many tiny lines at the corners of his eyes, and a general sallowness to his skin, indicated that he was older. Even this, though, lent no clue to the truth. Thomas Lloyd had been born in 1881, and was now approaching sixty.

He took his watch from his waistcoat pocket, and saw that the time was a little after twelve. He turned to walk towards the pub on the Isleworth road, but then noticed a man standing by himself on the path beside the river. Even wearing the sunglasses, which filtered away the more intrusive reminders of past and future, Lloyd could see that it was one of the men he called freezers. This was a young man, rather plump and with prematurely balding hair. He had seen Lloyd, for as Lloyd looked down at him the young man turned ostentatiously away. Lloyd had nothing now to fear from the freezers, but they were always about and their presence never failed to make him uneasy.

Far away, in the direction of Barnes, Lloyd could hear another air-raid siren droning out its warning.

June, 1903
The world was at peace, and the weather was warm. Thomas James Lloyd, recently down from Cambridge, twenty-one years of age, mustachioed, light of tread, walked gaily through the trees that grew across the side of Richmond Hill.

It was a Sunday and there were many people about. Earlier in the day Thomas had attended church with his father and mother and sister, sitting in the pew that was reserved traditionally for the Lloyds of Richmond. The house on the Hill had belonged to the family for more than two hundred years, and William Lloyd, the present head of the family, owned most of the houses on the Sheen side of town as well as administering one of the largest businesses in the whole of Surrey. A family of substance indeed, and Thomas James Lloyd lived in the knowledge that one day the substance would be his by inheritance.

Worldly matters thus ensured, Thomas felt free to divert his attention to activities of a more important nature; namely, Charlotte Carrington and her sister Sarah.

That one day he would marry one of the two sisters had been an inevitability long acknowledged by both families, although precisely which of the two it would be had been occupying his thoughts for many weeks.

There was much to choose between the two—or so Thomas himself considered—but if his choice had been free, then his mind would have been at rest. Unfortunately for him it had been made plain by the girls' parents that it would be Charlotte who would make the better wife for a future industrialist and landowner, and in many ways this was so. The difficulty arose because Thomas had fallen impetuously for her younger sister Sarah, a state of affairs of absolutely no moment to Mrs. Carrington.

Charlotte, twenty years of age, was an undeniably handsome girl, and Thomas much enjoyed her company. She appeared to be prepared to accept a proposal of marriage from him, and to be fair she was endowed with much grace and intelligence, but whenever they had been together neither had had much of interest to say to the other. Charlotte was an ambitious and emancipated girl—for so she styled herself—and was constantly reading historical tracts. Her one consuming interest was in touring the various churches of Surrey to take brass-rubbings from the plates there. Thomas, a liberal and understanding young man, was pleased she had found a hobby, but could not own to any mutual interest.

Sarah Carrington was an altogether different proposition. Two years younger than her sister, and thus, by her mother's estimation, not yet eligible for marriage (or not, at least, until a husband had been found for Charlotte), Sarah was at once a person to be coveted by virtue of her unavailability and yet also a delightful personality in her own right. When Thomas had first paid visits to Charlotte, Sarah was still being finished at school, but by astute questioning of Charlotte and his own sister, Thomas had discovered that Sarah liked to play tennis and croquet, was a keen bicyclist, and was acquainted with all the latest dance steps. A surreptitious glance into the family's photographic album had established that she was also astoundingly beautiful. This last aspect of her he had confirmed for himself at their first meeting, and he had promptly fallen in love with her. Since then he had contrived to transfer his attentions, and with no small measure of success. Twice already he had spoken to her alone . . . no minor achievement when one considered the enthusiasm with which Mrs. Carrington encouraged Thomas always to be with Charlotte. Once he had been left alone with Sarah for a few minutes in the Carringtons' drawing room, and on the second occasion he had managed a few words with her during a family picnic. Even on this brief acquaintance, Thomas had become convinced that he would settle for no less a wife than Sarah.

So it was that on this Sunday Thomas's mood was full of light, for by a most agreeable contrivance he had ensured himself at least an hour alone with Sarah.

The instrument of this contrivance was one Waring Lloyd, a cousin of his. Waring had always seemed to Thomas a most unconscionable oaf, but remembering that Charlotte had once remarked on him (and feeling that each would be eminently suited to the other), Thomas had proposed a riverside stroll for the afternoon. Waring, suitably confided in, would delay Charlotte while they walked, so allowing Thomas and Sarah to go on ahead.

Thomas was several minutes early for the rendezvous, and paced to and fro good-naturedly while waiting for his cousin. It was cooler by the river, for the trees grew right down to the water's edge, and several of the ladies walking along the path behind the boathouse had folded their parasols and were clutching shawls about their shoulders.

When at last Waring appeared, the two cousins greeted each other amiably—more so than at any time in the recent past—and debated whether they should cross by the ferry, or walk the long way around by the bridge. There was still plenty of time in hand, so they opted for the latter course.

Thomas once again reminded Waring of what was to happen during the stroll, and Waring confirmed that he understood. The arrangement was no sacrifice to him, for he found Charlotte no less delightful than Sarah, and would doubtless find much to say to the older girl.

Later, as they crossed Richmond Bridge to the Middlesex side of the river, Thomas paused, resting his hands on the stone parapet of the bridge. He was watching four young men struggling ineptly with a punt, trying to maneuver it against the stream towards the side, while on the bank two older men shouted conflicting instructions.

August, 1940
"You'd better take cover, sir. Just in case."

Thomas Lloyd was startled by the voice at his side, and he turned. It was an air-raid warden, an elderly man in a dark uniform. On his shoulder, and stenciled on his metal helmet, were the letters A.R.P. In spite of his polite tone of voice he was looking suspiciously at Lloyd. The part-time work Lloyd had been doing in Richmond paid barely enough for food and lodgings, and what little spare there was usually went on drink; he was still wearing substantially the same clothes as he had five years ago, and they were the worse for wear.

"Is there going to be a raid?" Lloyd said.

"Never can tell. Jerry's still bombing the ports, but he'll start on the towns any day now."

They both glanced towards the sky in the southeast. There, high in the blue, were several white vapor trails curling, but no other evidence of the German bombers everyone so feared.

"I'll be safe," Lloyd said. "I'm going for a walk. I'll be away from the houses if a raid starts."

"That's all right, sir. If you meet anyone else out there, remind them there's an alert on."

"I'll do that."

The warden nodded to him, then walked slowly towards the town. Lloyd raised his sunglasses for a moment and watched him.

A few yards from where they had been standing was one of the freezers' tableaux: two men and a woman. When he had first noticed this tableau Lloyd had inspected the people carefully, and had judged by their clothes that they must have been frozen at some time in the mid-nineteenth century. This tableau was the oldest he had so far discovered, and as such was of special interest to him. He had learned that the moment of a tableau's erosion was unpredictable. Some tableaux lasted for several years, others only a day or two. The fact that this one had survived for at least ninety years indicated just how erratic the erosions were.

The three frozen people were halted in their walk directly in front of the warden, who hobbled along the pavement towards them. As he reached them he showed no sign of awareness, and in a moment had passed right through them.

Lloyd lowered his sunglasses, and the image of the three people became vague and ill-defined.

June, 1903
When Waring's prospects were compared with those of Thomas they seemed unremarkable, but by normal standards they were nonetheless considerable. Accordingly, Mrs. Carrington (who knew more about the distribution of the Lloyd wealth than anyone outside immediate family circles) greeted Waring with civility.

The two young men were offered a glass of cold lemon tea, and then asked for their opinion on some matter concerning an herbaceous border. Thomas, by now well used to Mrs. Carrington's small talk, couched his reply in a few words, but Waring, anxious to please, set forth into a detailed response. He was still speaking knowledgeably of replanting and bedding when the girls appeared. They walked out through the French window and came across the lawn towards them.

Seen together it was obvious that the two were sisters, but to Thomas's eager eye one girl's beauty easily outshone the other's. Charlotte's expression was more earnest, and her bearing more practical. Sarah affected a modesty and timorousness (although Thomas knew it to be just an affectation), and her smile when she saw the young men was enough to convince Thomas that from this moment his life would be an eternity of summer.

Twenty minutes passed while the four young people and the girls' mother walked about the garden. Thomas, at first impatient to put his scheme to the test, managed after a few minutes to control himself. He had noticed that both Mrs. Carrington and Charlotte were amused by Waring's conversation, and this was an unexpected bonus. After all, the whole afternoon lay ahead, and these minutes were being well spent!

At last they were released from their courtesies, and the four set off for their planned stroll.

The girls each carried a sunshade: Charlotte's was white, Sarah's was pink. As they went through the grounds towards the riverside walk the girls' dresses rustled on the long grass, although Charlotte raised her skirt a little, for she said that the grass so stained cotton.

Approaching the river they heard the sounds of other people: children calling, a girl and a man from the town laughing together, and a rowing-eight striking in unison to the cox's instructions. As they came to the riverside path, and the two young men helped the girls over a stile, a mongrel dog leaped out of the water some twenty yards away and shook itself with great gusto.

The path was not wide enough for them to walk abreast, and so Thomas and Sarah took the lead. Just once he was able to catch Waring's eye, and the other gave the slightest of nods.

A few minutes later, Waring delayed Charlotte to show her a swan and some cygnets swimming by the reeds, and Thomas and Sarah walked slowly on ahead.

By now they were some distance from the town, and meadows lay on either side of the river.

August, 1940
The pub was set back a short distance from the road, with an area in front of it laid with paving stones. On these, before the war, there had been five circular metal tables where one could drink in the open air, but they had been removed for scrap-iron during the last winter. Apart from this, and the fact that the

windows had been criss-crossed with tape in Home-Office-approved fashion, to prevent glass splinters flying, there was no outward sign that business was not normal.

Inside Lloyd ordered a pint of bitter, and took it with him to one of the tables.

He sipped the drink, then regarded the other occupants of the bar.

Apart from himself and the barmaid there were four other people present. Two men sat morosely together at one table, half-empty glasses of stout before them. Another man sat alone at a table by the door. He had a newspaper on the table before him, and was staring at the crossword.

The fourth person, who stood against one of the walls, was a freezer. This one, Lloyd noted, was a woman. She, like the men freezers, wore a drab gray overall, and held one of the freeze instruments. This was shaped rather like a modern portable camera, and was carried on a lanyard strung around the neck, but it was much larger than a camera and was approximately cubical in shape. At the front, where on a camera would be a viewfinder and lens, there was a rectangular strip of white glass, apparently opaque or translucent, and it was through this that the freezing-beam was projected.

Lloyd, still wearing his dark glasses, could only just see the woman. She did not seem to be looking in his direction, but after a few seconds she stepped back through the wall and disappeared from his sight.

He noticed that the barmaid was watching him, and as soon as she had caught his eye she spoke to him.

"D'you think they're coming this time?"

"I shouldn't care to speculate," Lloyd said, not wishing to be drawn into conversation. He took several mouthfuls of the beer, wanting to finish it and be on his way.

"These sirens have ruined the trade," the barmaid said. "One after the other, all day and sometimes in the evenings too. And it's always a false alarm."

"Yes," Lloyd said.

She continued with her complaints for a few more seconds, but then someone called her from the other bar and she went to serve him. Lloyd was greatly relieved, for he disliked speaking to people here. He had felt isolated for too long, and had never mastered the modern way of conversation. Quite often he was misunderstood, for it was his way to speak in the more formal manner of his own contemporaries.

He was regretting having delayed. This would have been a good time to go to the meadows, for while the air-raid alert was on there would be only a few people about. He disliked not being alone when he walked by the river.

He drank the rest of his beer, then stood up and walked towards the door.

As he did so he noticed for the first time that there was a recent tableau by the door. He did not seek out the tableaux, for he found their presence disturbing, but new ones were nevertheless of interest.

There were two men and a woman seeming to sit at a table; the image of them was indistinct, and so Lloyd took off his sunglasses. At once the brilliance of the tableau surprised him, seeming to overshadow the man who still sat regarding his crossword at the far end of the table.

One of the two frozen men was younger than the other two people, and he sat slightly apart. He was smoking, for a cigarette lay on the edge of the table, the end overhanging the wooden surface by a few millimeters. The older man and the woman were together, for the woman's hand was held in the man's, and he was bending forward to kiss her wrist. His lips rested on her arm, and his eyes were closed. The woman, still slim and attractive although apparently well into her forties, seemed amused by this for she was smiling, but she was not watching her friend. Instead, she was looking across the table at the younger man, who, beer glass raised to his mouth, was watching the kiss with interest. On the table between them was the man's untouched glass of bitter, and the woman's glass of port. They had been eating potato crisps, for a crumpled paper bag and the blue salt-packet lay in the ashtray. The smoke from the young man's cigarette, gray and curling, was motionless in the air, and a piece of ash, falling towards the ground, hovered a few inches above the carpet.

"You want something, mate?" It was the man with the crossword.

Lloyd put on his sunglasses again with unseemly haste, realizing that for the last few seconds he had been seeming to stare at the man.

"I beg your pardon," he said, and fell back on the excuse he gave when such embarrassments occurred. "I thought for a moment I recognized you."

The man peered myopically up at him. "Never seen you before in my life."

Lloyd affected a vacant nod, and passed on towards the door. For a moment he caught a glimpse again of the three frozen victims. The young man with the beer glass, watching coolly; the man kissing, bent over so that his upper body was almost horizontal; the woman smiling, watching the young man and enjoying the attention she was being paid; the cigarette smoke static.

Lloyd went through the door, and into the sunshine.

June, 1903

"Your mama wishes me to marry your sister," Thomas said.

"I know. It is not what Charlotte desires."

"Nor I. May I inquire as to your feelings on the matter?"

"I am in accord, Thomas."

They were walking along slowly, about three feet apart from each other. Both stared at the gravel of the path as they walked, not meeting the other's eyes. Sarah was turning her parasol through her fingers, causing the tassels to swirl and tangle. Now they were in the riverside meadows they were almost alone, although Waring and Charlotte were following about two hundred yards behind.

"Would you say that we were strangers, Sarah?"

"By what standards do you mean?" She had paused a little before responding.

"Well, for instance, this is the first occasion on which we have been allowed any degree of intimacy together."

"And that by a contrivance," Sarah said.

"What do you mean?"

"I saw you signal to your cousin."

Thomas felt himself go a little red, but he considered that in the brightness and warmth of the afternoon a flush would go unnoticed. On the river the rowing-eight had turned, and were now passing them again.

After a few moments, Sarah said: "I am not avoiding your question, Thomas. I am considering whether or not we are strangers."

"Then what do you say?"

"I think we know each other a little."

"I should be glad to see you again, Sarah. Without the need for contrivance, that is."

"Charlotte and I will speak to Mama. You have already been much discussed, Thomas, although not as yet with Mama. You need not fear for hurting my sister's feelings, for although she likes you she does not yet feel ready for marriage."

Thomas, his pulse racing, felt a rush of confidence within him.

"And you, Sarah?" he said. "May I continue to court you?"

She turned away from him then, and stepped through the long grass beside the edge of the path. He saw the long sweep of her skirt, and the shining pink circle of her parasol. Her left hand dangled at her side, brushing lightly against her skirt.

She said: "I find your advances most welcome, Thomas."

Her voice was faint, but the words reached his ears as if she had pronounced them clearly in a silent room.

Thomas's response was immediate. He swept his boater from his head, and opened his arms wide.

"My dearest Sarah," he cried. "Will you marry me?"

She turned to face him and for a moment she was still,

regarding him seriously. Her parasol rested on her shoulder, no longer turning. Then, seeeing that he was in earnest, she smiled a little, and Thomas saw that she too had allowed a blush of pink to color her cheeks.

"Yes, of course I will," Sarah said.

She stepped towards him extending her left hand, and Thomas, his straw hat still held high, reached forward with his right hand to take hers.

Neither Thomas nor Sarah could have seen that in that moment a man had stepped forward from beside the water's edge, and was leveling at them a small black instrument.

August, 1940
The all-clear had not sounded, but the town seemed to be returning to life. Traffic was crossing Richmond Bridge, and a short distance down the road towards Isleworth a queue was forming outside a grocer's shop while a delivery van was parked alongside the curb. Now that he was at last setting off on his daily walk, Thomas Lloyd felt more at ease with the tableaux, and he took off his dark glasses for the last time and returned them to their case.

In the center of the bridge was the overturning carriage. The driver, a gaunt middle-aged man wearing a green coat and shiny black top hat, had his left arm raised. In his hand he was holding the whip, and the lash snaked up over the bridge in a graceful curve. His right hand was already releasing the reins, and was reaching forward towards the hard road surface in a desperate attempt to soften the impact of his fall. In the open compartment at the rear was an elderly lady, much powdered and veiled, wearing a black velvet coat. She had been thrown sideways from her seat as the wheel axle broke, and was holding up her hands in fright. Of the two horses in harness, one was apparently unaware of the accident, and had been frozen in mid-stride. The other, though, had tossed back its head and raised both its forelegs. Its nostrils were flaring, and behind the blinkers its eyes were rolled back.

As Lloyd crossed the road a red G.P.O. van drove through the tableau, the driver quite aware of its presence.

Two of the freezers were waiting at the top of the shallow ramp which led down to the riverside walk, and as Lloyd turned to follow the path towards the distant meadows, the two men walked a short distance behind him.

June, 1903, to January, 1935

The summer's day, with its two young lovers imprisoned, became a moment extended.

Thomas James Lloyd, straw hat raised in his left hand, his other hand reaching out. His right knee was slightly bent, as if he were about to kneel, and his face was full of happiness and expectation. A breeze seemed to be ruffling his hair, for three strands stood on end, but these had been dislodged when he removed his hat. A tiny winged insect, which had settled on his lapel, was frozen in its moment of flight, an instinct to escape too late.

A short distance away stood Sarah Carrington. The sun fell across her face, highlighting the locks of auburn hair that fell from beneath her bonnet. One foot, stepping towards Thomas, showed itself beneath the hem of her skirt, shod in a buttoned boot. Her right hand was lifting a pink parasol away from her shoulder, as if she were about to wave it in joy. She was laughing, and her eyes, soft and brown, gazed with affection at the young man before her.

Their hands were extended towards each other's. Sarah's left hand was an inch from his right, her fingers already curling in anticipation of holding his.

Thomas's fingers, reaching out, revealed by irregular white patches that until an instant before his fists had been clenched in anxious tension.

The whole: the long grass moist after a shower a few hours before, the pale brown gravel of the path, the wildflowers that grew in the meadow, the adder that basked not four feet from the couple, the clothes, their skin . . . all were rendered in colors bleached and saturated with preternatural luminosity.

August, 1940
There was a sound of aircraft in the air.

Although aircraft were unknown in his time, Thomas Lloyd had now grown accustomed to them. He understood that before the war there had been civilian aircraft, but he had never seen any of these, and since then the only ones he had seen were warplanes. Like everyone else of the time he was familiar with the sight of the high black shapes, and with the curious droning, throbbing sound of the enemy bombers. Each day air battles were being fought over southeast England; sometimes the bombers evaded the fighters, sometimes not.

He glanced up at the sky. While he had been inside the pub, the vapor trails he had seen earlier had disappeared; a new pattern of white had appeared, however, more recently made, farther to the north.

Lloyd walked down the Middlesex side of the river. Looking directly across the river he saw how the town had been extended since his day: on the Surrey side of the river the trees which had once concealed the houses were mostly gone, and in their place were shops and offices. On this side, where houses had been set back from the river, more had been built close to the bank. As far as he could see, only the wooden boathouse had survived intact from his time, and that was badly in need of a coat of paint.

He was at the focus of past, present and future: only the boathouse and the river itself were as clearly defined as he. The freezers, from some unknown period of the future, as ethereal to ordinary men as their wishful dreams, moved like shadows through light, stealing sudden moments with their incomprehensible devices. The tableaux themselves, frozen, isolated, insubstantial, waiting in an eternity of silence for those people of the future generation to see them.

Encompassing all was a turbulent present, obsessed with war.

Thomas Lloyd, of neither past nor present, saw himself as a product of both, and a victim of the future.

Then, from high above the town, there came the sound of an explosion and a roar of engines, and the present impinged on Lloyd's consciousness. A British fighter plane banked away towards the south, and a German bomber fell burning towards the ground. After a few seconds two men escaped from the aircraft, and their parachutes opened.

January, 1935

As if waking from a dream, Thomas experienced a moment of recall and recognition, but in an instant it was gone.

He saw Sarah before him, reaching towards him; he saw the bright garishness of the heightened colors; he saw the stillness of the frozen summer's day.

It faded as he looked, and he cried out Sarah's name. She made no move or reply, stayed immobile, and the light around her darkened.

Thomas pitched forward, a great weakness overcoming his limbs, and he fell to the ground.

It was night, and snow lay thickly on the meadows beside the Thames.

August, 1940

Until the moment of its final impact, the bomber fell in virtual silence. Both engines had stopped, although only one was on fire, and flame and smoke poured from the fuselage, leaving behind a thick black trail across the sky. The plane crashed by the bend in the river, and there was a huge explosion. Meanwhile, the two Germans who had escaped from the aircraft drifted down across Richmond Hill, swaying beneath their parachutes.

Lloyd shaded his eyes with his hands, and watched to see where they would land. One had been carried farther by the aircraft before jumping and was much nearer, falling slowly towards the river.

The Civil Defense authorities in the town were evidently alert, for within a few months of the parachutes' appearing, Lloyd heard the sound of police- and fire-bells.

There was a movement a short distance from Lloyd, and he turned. The two freezers who had been following him had been joined by two others, one of whom was the woman he had seen inside the pub. The freezer who seemed to be the youngest had already raised his device, and was pointing it across the river, but the other three were saying something to him. (Lloyd could see their lips moving, and the expressions on their faces, but, as always, he could not hear them.) The young man shrugged away the restraining hand of one of the others, and walked down the bank to the edge of the water.

One of the Germans came down near the edge of Richmond Park and was lost to sight as he fell beyond the houses built near the crest of the Hill; the other, buoyed up temporarily by a sudden updraught, drifted out across the river itself, and was now only some fifty feet in the air. Lloyd could see the German aviator pulling on the cords of his parachute, trying desperately to steer himself towards the bank. As air spilled from the white shroud, he fell more quickly.

The young freezer by the edge of the river was leveling his device, apparently aiming it with the aid of a reflex sight built into the instrument. A moment later the German's efforts to save himself from falling into the water were rewarded in a way he could never have anticipated: ten feet above the surface of the water, his knees raised to take the brunt of the impact, one arm waving, the German was frozen in flight.

The freezer lowered his instrument, and Lloyd stared across the water at the hapless man suspended in the air.

January, 1935
The tranformation of a summer's day into a winter's night was the least of the changes that Thomas Lloyd discovered on

regaining consciousness. In what had been for him a few seconds he had moved from a world of stability, peace and prosperity to one where dynamic and violent situations obtained. In that same short moment of time, he himself had lost the security of his ensured future, and become a pauper. Most traumatically of all, he had never been allowed to take to its fruition the surge of love he had felt for Sarah.

Night was the only relief from the tableaux, and Sarah was still held in frozen time.

He recovered consciousness shortly before dawn, and, not understanding what had happened to him, walked slowly back towards Richmond town. The sun had risen shortly after, and as light struck the tableaux that littered the paths and roads, and as it struck the freezers who constantly moved in their half-world of intrusive futurity, Lloyd realized neither that in these lay the cause of his own predicament, nor that his perception of the images was itself a product of his experience.

In Richmond he was found by a policeman, and was taken to a hospital. Here, treated for the pneumonia he had contracted as he lay in the snow, and later for the amnesia that seemed the only explanation for his condition, Thomas Lloyd saw the freezers moving through the wards and corridors. The tableaux were here too: a dying man falling from his bed; a young nurse—dressed in the uniform of fifty years before—frozen as she walked from a ward, a deep frown creasing her brow; a child throwing a ball in the garden by the convalescent wing.

As he was nursed back to physical health, Lloyd became obsessed with a need to return to the meadows by the river, and before he was fully recovered he discharged himself and went directly there.

By then the snow had melted, but the weather was still cold and a white frost lay on the ground. Out by the river, where a bank of grass grew thickly beside the path, was a frozen moment of summer, and in its midst was Sarah.

He could see her, but she could not see him; he could take the hand that was rightly his to take, but his fingers would pass through the illusion; he could walk around her, seeming to step through the green summer grasses, and feel the cold of the frozen soil penetrating the thin soles of his shoes.

And as night fell so the moment of the past became invisible, and Thomas was relieved of the agony of the vision.

Time passed, but there was never a day when he did not walk along the riverside path, and stand again before the image of Sarah, and reach out to take her hand.

August, 1940
The German parachutist hung above the river, and Lloyd looked again at the freezers. They were apparently still criticizing the youngest of them for his action, and yet seemed fascinated with his result. It was certainly one of the most dramatic tableaux Lloyd himself had seen.

Now that the man had been frozen it was possible to see that his eyes were tightly closed, and that he was holding his nose with his fingers in anticipation of his plunge. In addition, it now became clear that he had been wounded in the aircraft, because blood was staining his flying-jacket. The tableau was at once amusing and poignant, a reminder to Lloyd that, however unreal this present might be to him, it was no illusion to the people of the time.

In a moment Lloyd understood the particular interest of the freezers in this unfortunate airman, for without warning the pocket of frozen time eroded and the young German plunged into the river. The parachute billowed and folded in on top of him. As he surfaced he thrashed his arms wildly, trying to free himself of the constraining cords.

It was not the first time Lloyd had seen a tableau erode, but he had never before seen it happen so soon after freezing. It had always seemed to him a matter of chance, but having seen the distance from which the beam had been released—the airman had been at least fifty yards away—he surmised that the time a tableau survived was probably dependent on how close the subject was to the freezer. (He himself had escaped from his own tableau; had Sarah been nearer the freezer when the beam was released?)

In the center of the river the German had succeeded in freeing himself of the parachute, and was swimming slowly towards the opposite bank. His descent must have been observed by the authorities, because even before he reached the sloping landing stage of the boathouse, four policemen had appeared from the direction of the road, and helped him out of the water. He made no attempt to resist capture but lay weakly on the ground, awaiting the arrival of an ambulance.

Lloyd remembered the only other time he had seen a tableau erode quickly. A freezer had acted to prevent a traffic accident: a man stepping carelessly into the path of a car had been frozen in mid-step. Although the driver of the car had stopped abruptly, and had looked around in amazement for the man he thought he had been about to kill, he had evidently assumed that he had imagined the incident, for he eventually drove off again. Only Lloyd, with his ability to see the tableau, could still see the man: stepping back, arms flailing in terror, still seeing too late the oncoming vehicle. Three days later, when Lloyd returned to the place, the tableau had eroded and the man was gone. He, like Lloyd—and now the German aviator—would be moving through a half-world, one where past, present and future co-existed uneasily.

Lloyd watched the shroud of the parachute drift along the river until at last it sank, and then turned away to continue his walk to the meadows. As he did so he realized that even more of the freezers had appeared on this side of the river, and were walking behind him, following him.

As he reached the bend in the river, from which point he always gained his first sight of Sarah, he saw that the bomber had crashed in the meadows. The explosion of its impact had set fire to the grass, and the smoke from this, together with that from the burning wreckage, obscured his view.

January, 1935, to August, 1940
Thomas Lloyd never again left Richmond. He lived inexpensively, found occasional work, tried not to be outstanding in any way.

What of the past? He discovered that on June 22, 1903, his apparent disappearance with Sarah had led to the conclusion that he had absconded with her. His father, William Lloyd, head of the noted Richmond family, had disowned him. Colonel and Mrs. Carrington had announced a reward for his arrest, but in 1910 they had moved away from the area. Thomas also discovered that his cousin Waring had never married Charlotte, and that he had emigrated to Australia. His own parents were both dead, there was no means of tracing his sister, and the family home had been sold and demolished.

(On the day he read the files of the local newspaper, he stood with Sarah, overcome with grief.)

What of the future? It was pervasive, intrusive. It existed on a plane where only those who were frozen and released could sense it. It existed in the form of men who came to freeze the images of the present.

(On the day he first understood what the shadowy men he called freezers might be, he stood beside Sarah, staring around protectively. That day, as if sensing Lloyd's realization, one of the freezers had walked along the riverbank, watching the young man and his time-locked sweetheart.)

What of the present? Lloyd neither cared for the present nor shared it with its occupants. It was violent, alien, frightening. The machines and men were threatening. It was, to him, as vague a presence as the other two dimensions. Only the past and its frozen images were real.

(On the day he first saw a tableau erode he ran all the way to the meadows, and stood long into the evening, trying ceaselessly for the first sign of substance in Sarah's outstretched hand.)

August, 1940

Only in the riverside meadows, where the town was distant and the houses were concealed by trees, did Thomas ever feel at one with the present. Here past and present fused, for little had changed since his day. Here he could stand before the image of Sarah and fancy himself still on that summer's day in 1903, still the young man with raised straw hat and slightly bended knee. Here too he rarely saw any of the freezers, and the few tableaux visible (farther along the walk an elderly fisherman had been time-locked as he pulled a trout from the stream; towards the distant houses of Twickenham, a little boy in a sailor suit walked sulkily with his nanny) could be accepted as a natural part of the world he had known.

Today, though, the present had intruded violently. The exploding bomber had scattered fragments of itself across the meadows. Black smoke from the wreckage spread in an oily cloud across the river, and the smoldering grass poured white smoke to drift beside it. Much of the ground had already been blackened by fire.

Sarah was invisible to him, lost somewhere in the smoke.

Thomas paused, and took a kerchief from his pocket. He stooped by the river's edge and soaked it in the water, then, after wringing it out, he held it over his nose and mouth.

He glanced behind him and saw that there were now eight of the freezers with him. They were paying no attention to him, and walked on while he prepared himself, insensible to the smoke. They passed through the burning grass, and walked towards the main concentration of wreckage. One of the freezers was already making some kind of adjustment to his device.

A breeze had sprung up in the last few minutes, and it caused the smoke to move away smartly from the fires, staying lower on the ground. As this happened, Thomas saw the image of Sarah above the smoke. He hurried towards her, alarmed by the proximity of the burning aircraft, even as he knew that neither fire, explosion nor smoke could harm her.

His feet threw up smoldering grasses as he went towards her, and at times the variable wind caused the smoke to swirl about his head. His eyes were watering, and although his wetted kerchief acted as a partial filter against the grass smoke, when the oily fumes from the aircraft gusted around him he choked and gagged on the acrid vapors.

At length he decided to wait; Sarah was safe inside her cocoon of frozen time, and there was no conceivable point to his suffocating simply to be with her, when in a few minutes the fire would burn itself out.

He retreated to the edge of the burning area, rinsed out his kerchief in the river, and sat down to wait.

The freezers were exploring the wreckage with the greatest interest, apparently drifting through the flames and smoke to enter the deepest parts of the conflagration.

There came the sound of a bell away to Thomas's right, and in a moment a fire-tender halted in the narrow lane that ran along the distant edge of the meadows. Several firemen climbed down, and stood looking across the field at the wreckage. At this Thomas's heart sank, for he realized what was to follow. He had sometimes seen photographs in the newspapers of crashed German aircraft; they were invariably placed under military guard until the pieces could be taken away for examination. If this were to happen here it would deny him access to Sarah for several days.

For the moment, though, he would still have a chance to be with her. He was too far away to hear what the firemen were saying, but it looked as if no attempt was going to be made to put out the fire. Smoke still poured from the fuselage, but the flames had died down, and most of the smoke was coming from the grass. With no houses in the vicinity, and with the wind blowing towards the river, there was little likelihood the fire would spread.

He stood up again, and walked quickly towards Sarah.

In a few moments he had reached her, and she stood before him: eyes shining in the sunlight, parasol lifting, arm extending. She was in a sphere of safety; although smoke blew through her, the grasses on which she stood were green and moist and cool. As he had done every day for more than five years, Thomas stood facing her and waited for a sign of the erosion of her tableau. He stepped, as he had frequently done before, into the area of the time-freeze. Here, although his foot appeared to press on the grasses of 1903, a flame curled around his leg and he was forced to step back quickly.

Thomas saw some of the freezers coming towards him. They had apparently inspected the wreckage to their satisfaction, and judged none of it worth preserving in a time-freeze. Thomas tried to disregard them, but their sinister silence could not be forgotten easily.

The smoke poured about him, rich and heady with the smells of burning grass, and he looked again at Sarah. Just as time had frozen about her in that moment, so it had frozen about his love for her. Time had not diminished, it had preserved.

The freezers were watching him. Thomas saw that the eight vague figures, standing not ten feet away from him, were looking at him with interest. Then, on the far side of the meadow, one of the firemen shouted something at him. He would seem to be standing here alone; no one could see the tableaux, no one knew of the freezers. The fireman walked towards him, waving an arm, telling him to move away. It would take him a minute or more to reach them, and that was time enough for Thomas.

One of the freezers stepped forward, and in the heart of the smoke Thomas saw the captured summer begin to dim. Smoke curled up around Sarah's feet, and flame licked through the moist, time-frozen grasses around her ankles. He saw the fabric at the bottom of her skirt begin to scorch.

And her hand, extended towards him, lowered.

The parasol fell to the ground.

Sarah's head drooped forward, but immediately she was conscious . . . and the step towards him, commenced thirty-seven years before, was concluded.

"Thomas?" Her voice was clear, untouched.

He rushed towards her.

"Thomas! The smoke! What is happening?"
"Sarah . . . my love!"

As she went into his arms he realized that her skirt had taken fire, but he placed his arms around her shoulders and hugged her intimately and tenderly. He could feel her cheek, still warm from the blush of so long ago, nestling against his. Her hair, falling loose beneath her bonnet, lay across his face, and the pressure of her arms around his waist was no less than that of his own.

Dimly, he saw a gray movement beyond them, and in a moment the noises were stilled and the smoke ceased to swirl. The flame which had taken purchase on the hem of her skirt now died, and the summer sun which warmed them shone lightly in the tableau. Past and future became one, the present faded, life stilled, life for ever.

THE KING'S WISHES
ROBERT SHECKLEY

Robert Sheckley burst into the science-fiction world with frantic energy about 1952, scattering dazzling and high-spirited short stories in all directions at a phenomenal rate. His clear, cool style, his unfailing comic touch, his lunatic inventiveness made him an immediate favorite, and this sly, playful story is a fair sample of his work. The American-born Sheckley has lived in Europe a long while and has been relatively inactive as a writer after those early busy years, but he writes now from London that he is once more keeping his typewriter humming—good news for all science-fiction readers except those who believe the stuff has to be dignified and stately and dreadfully serious.

After squatting behind a glassware display for almost two hours, Bob Granger felt his legs begin to cramp. He moved to ease them, and his number-ten iron slipped off his lap, clattering on the floor.

"Shh," Janice whispered, her mashie gripped tightly.

"I don't think he's going to come," Bob said.

"Be quiet, honey," Janice whispered again, peering into the darkness of their store.

There was no sign of the burglar yet. He had come every

night in the past week, mysteriously removing generators, refrigerators and air conditioners. Mysteriously—for he tampered with no locks, jimmied no windows, left no footprints. Yet somehow, he was able to sneak in, time after time, and slink out with a good part of their stock.

"I don't think this was such a good idea," Bob whispered. "After all, a man capable of carrying several hundred pounds of generator on his back—"

"We'll handle him," Janice said, with the certainty that had made her a master sergeant in the WAC Motor Corps. "Besides, we have to stop him—he's postponing our wedding day."

Bob nodded in the darkness. He and Janice had built and stocked the Country Department Store with their army savings. They were planning on getting married, as soon as the profits enabled them to. But when someone stole refrigerators and air conditioners—

"I think I hear something," Janice said, shifting her grip on the mashie.

There was a faint noise somewhere in the store. They waited. Then they heard the sound of feet, padding over the linoleum.

"When he gets to the middle of the floor," Janice whispered, "switch on the lights."

Finally they were able to make out a blackness against the lesser blackness of the store. Bob switched on the lights, shouting, "Hold it there!"

"Oh, no!" Janice gasped, almost dropping her mashie. Bob turned and gulped.

Standing in front of them was a being at least ten feet tall. He had budding horns on his forehead, and tiny wings on his back. He was dressed in a pair of dungarees and a white sweat shirt with EBLIS TECH written across it in scarlet letters. Scuffed white buckskins were on his tremendous feet, and he had a blond crewcut.

"Damn," he said, looking at Bob and Janice. "Knew I should have taken Invisibility in college." He wrapped his arms around his stomach and puffed out his cheeks. Instantly his legs disappeared. Puffing out his cheeks still more, he was able to make his stomach vanish. But that was as far as it went.

"Can't do it," he said, releasing his stored-up air. His stomach and legs came back into visibility. "Haven't got the knack. Damn."

"What do you want?" Janice asked, drawing herself to her full slender five foot three.

"Want? Let me see. Oh, yes. The fan." He walked across the room and picked up a large floor fan.

"Just a minute," Bob shouted. He walked up to the giant, his golf club poised. Janice followed close behind him. "Where do you think you're going with that?"

"To King Alerian," the giant said. "He wished for it."

"Oh, he did, did he?" Janice said. "Better put it down." She poised the mashie over her shoulder.

"But I *can't*," the young giant said, his tiny wings twitching nervously. "It's been wished for."

"You asked for it," Janice said. Although small, she was in fine condition from the WAC's, where she had spent her time repairing jeep engines. Now, blond hair flying, she swung her club.

"Ouch!" she said. The mashie bounced off the being's head, almost knocking Janice over with the recoil. At the same time, Bob swung his club at the giant's ribs.

It passed *through* the giant, ricocheting against the floor.

"Force is useless against a ferra," the young giant said apologetically.

"A what?" Bob asked.

"A ferra. We're first cousins of the jinn, and related by marriage to the devas." He started to walk back to the center of the room, the fan gripped in one broad hand. "Now if you'll excuse me—"

"A demon?" Janice stood openmouthed. Her parents had allowed no talk of ghosts or demons in the house, and Janice had grown up a hardheaded realist. She was skilled at repairing anything mechanical; that was her part of the partnership. But anything more fanciful she left to Bob.

Bob, having been raised on a liberal feeding of Oz and Burroughs, was more credulous. "You mean you're out of the *Arabian Nights?*" he asked.

"Oh, no," the ferra said. "The jinn of Arabia are my cousins, as I said. All demons are related, but I am a ferra, of the ferras."

"Would you mind telling me," Bob asked, "what you are doing with my generator, my air conditioner, and my refrigerator?"

"I'd be glad to," the ferra said, putting down the fan. He felt around the air, found what he wanted, and sat down on nothingness. Then he crossed his legs and tightened the laces of one buckskin.

"I graduated from Eblis Tech just about three weeks ago," he began. "And of course, I applied for civil service. I come from a long line of government men. Well, the lists were crowded, as they always are, so I—"

"Civil service?" Bob asked.

"Oh, yes. They're all civil-service jobs—even the jinni in Aladdin's lamp was a government man. You have to pass the tests, you know."

"Go on," Bob said.

"Well—promise this won't go any farther—I got my job through pull." He blushed orange. "My father is a ferra in the Underworld Council, so he used his influence. I was appointed over four thousand higher-ranking ferras, to the position of ferra of the King's Cup. That's quite an honor, you know."

There was a short silence. Then the ferra went on.

"I must confess I wasn't ready," he said sadly. "The ferra of the cup has to be skilled in all branches of demonology. I had just graduated from college—with only passing grades. But of course, I thought I could handle anything."

The ferra paused, and rearranged his body more comfortably on the air.

"But I don't want to bother you with my troubles," he said,

getting off the air and standing on the floor. "If you'll excuse me—" He picked up the fan.

"Just a minute," Janice said. "Has this king commanded you to get our fan?"

"In a way," the ferra said, turning orange again.

"Well, look," Janice said. "Is this king rich?" She had decided, for the moment, to treat this superstitious entity as a real person.

"He's a very wealthy monarch."

"Then why can't he buy this stuff?" Janice wanted to know. "Why does he have to steal it?"

"Well," the ferra mumbled, "there's no place where he can buy it."

"One of those backward Oriental countries," Janice said, half to herself.

"Why can't he import the goods? Any company would be glad to arrange it."

"This is all very embarrassing," the ferra said, rubbing one buckskin against another. "I wish I could make myself invisible."

"Out with it," Bob said.

"If you must know," the ferra said sullenly, "King Alerian lives in what you would call two thousand B.C."

"Then how—"

"Oh, just a minute," the young ferra said crossly. "I'll explain everything." He rubbed his perspiring hands on his sweat shirt.

"As I told you, I got the job of ferra of the King's Cup. Naturally, I expected the king would ask for jewels or beautiful women, either of which I could have supplied easily. We learn that in first-term conjuration. But the king had all the jewels he wanted, and more wives than he knew what to do with. So what does he do but say, 'Ferra, my palace is hot in the summer. Do that which will make my palace cool.'

"I knew right then I was in over my head. It takes an advanced ferra to handle climate. I guess I spent too much time on the track team. I was stuck.

"I hurried to the master encyclopedia and looked up "Climate." The spells were just too much for me. And of course, I couldn't ask for help. That would have been an admission of incompetence. But I read that there was artificial climate control in the twentieth century. So I walked here, along the narrow trail to the future, and took one of your air conditioners. When the king wanted me to stop his food from spoiling, I came back for a refrigerator. Then it was—"

"You hooked them all to the generator?" Janice asked, interested in such details.

"Yes. I may not be much with spells, but I'm pretty handy mechanically."

It made sense, Bob thought. After all, who could keep a palace cool in 2,000 B.C.? Not all the money in the world could buy the gust of icy air from an air conditioner, or the food-saving qualities of a refrigerator. But what still bothered Bob was, what kind of a demon was he? He didn't look Assyrian. Certainly not Egyptian . . .

"No, I don't get it," Janice said. "In the *past*? You mean time travel?"

"Sure. I majored in time travel," the ferra said, with a proud, boyish grin.

Aztec perhaps, Bob thought, although that seemed unlikely . . .

"Well," Janice said, "why don't you go somewhere else? Why not steal from one of the big department stores?"

"This is the only place the trail to the future leads," the ferra said.

He picked up the fan. "I'm sorry to be doing this, but if I don't make good here, I'll never get another appointment. It'll be limbo for me."

He disappeared.

Half an hour later, Bob and Janice were in a corner booth of an all-night diner, drinking black coffee and talking in low tones.

"I don't believe a word of it," Janice was saying, all her skepticism back in force. "Demons! Ferras!"

"You have to believe it," Bob said wearily. "You saw it."

"I don't have to believe everything I see," Janice said staunchly. Then she thought of the missing articles, the vanishing profits and the increasingly distant marriage. "All right," she said. "Oh, honey, what'll we do?"

"You have to fight magic with magic," Bob said confidently. "He'll be back tomorrow night. We'll be ready for him."

"I'm in favor of that," Janice said. "I know where we can borrow a Winchester—"

Bob shook his head. "Bullets will just bounce off him, or pass through. Good, strong magic, that's what we need. A dose of his own medicine."

"What kind of magic?" Janice asked.

"To play safe," Bob said, "we'd better use all kinds. I wish I knew where he's from. To be really effective, magic—"

"You want more coffee?" the counterman said, appearing suddenly in front of them.

Bob looked up guiltily. Janice blushed.

"Let's go," she said to Bob. "If anyone hears us, we'll be laughed out of town.

They met at the store that evening. Bob had spent the day at the library, gathering his materials. They consisted of twenty-five sheets covered on both sides with Bob's scrawling script.

"I still wish we had that Winchester," Janice said, picking up a tire iron from the hardware section.

At eleven forty-five, the ferra appeared.

"Hi," he said. "Where do you keep your electric heaters? The king wants something for winter. He's tired of open hearths. Too drafty."

"Begone," Bob said, "in the name of the cross!" He held up a cross.

"Sorry," the ferra said pleasantly. "The ferras aren't connected with Christianity."

"Begone in the name of Namtar and Idpa!" Bob went on, since Mesopotamia was first on his notes. "In the name of Utuq, dweller of the desert, in the name of Telal and Alal—"

"Oh, here they are," the ferra said. "Why do I get myself into these jams? This is the electric model, isn't it? Looks a little shoddy."

"I invoke Rata, the boatbuilder," Bob intoned, switching to Polynesia. "And Hina, the tapa maker."

"Shoddy nothing," Janice said, her business instincts getting the better of her. "That stove is guaranteed for a year. Unconditionally."

"I call on the Heavenly Wolf," Bob went on, moving into China when Polynesia had no effect. "The Wolf who guards the gates of Shang Ti. I invoke the thunder god, Lei Kung—"

"Let's see, I have an infrared broiler," the ferra said. "And I need a bathtub. Have you got a bathtub?"

"I call Bael, Buer, Forcas, Marchocias, Astaroth—"

"These are bathtubs, aren't they?" the ferra asked Janice, who nodded involuntarily. "I think I'll take the largest. The king is a good-sized man."

"—Behemoth, Theutus, Asmodeus and Incubus!" Bob finished. The ferra looked at him with respect.

Angrily Bob invoked Ormazd, Persian king of light, and then the Ammonitic Beelphegor, and Dagon of the ancient Philistines.

"That's all I can carry, I suppose," the ferra said.

Bob invoked Damballa. He called upon the gods of Arabia. He tried Thessalian magic, and spells from Asia Minor. He nudged Aztec gods and stirred Mayan spirits. He tried Africa, Madagascar, India, Ireland, Malaya, Scandinavia and Japan.

"That's impressive," the ferra said, "but it'll really do no good." He lifted the bathtub, broiler and heater.

"Why not?" Bob gasped, out of breath.

"You see, ferras are affected only by their own indigenous spells. Just as jinn are responsible only to magic laws of Arabia. Also, you don't know my true name, and I assure you, you can't do much of a job of exorcizing anything if you don't know its true name."

"What country are you from?" Bob asked, wiping perspiration from his forehead.

"Sorry," the ferra said. "But if you knew that, you might find the right spell to use against me. And I'm in enough trouble as it is."

"Now look," Janice said. "If the king is so rich, why can't he pay?"

"The king never pays for anything he can get free," the ferra said. "That's why he's so rich."

Bob and Janice glared at him, their marriage fading off into the future.

"See you tomorrow night," the ferra said.

He waved a friendly hand, and vanished.

"Well, now," Janice said, after the ferra had left. "What now? Any more bright ideas?"

"All out of them," Bob said, sitting down heavily on a sofa.

"Any more magic?" Janice asked, with a faint touch of irony.

"That won't work," Bob said. "I couldn't find *ferra* or *King Alerian* listed in any encyclopedia. He's probably from some place we'd never hear of. A little native state in India, perhaps."

"Just our luck," Janice said, abandoning irony. "What are we going to do? I suppose he'll want a vacuum cleaner next, and then a phonograph." She closed her eyes and concentrated.

"He really is trying to make good," Bob said.

"I think I have an idea," Janice said, opening her eyes.

"What's that?"

"First of all, it's *our* business that's important, and *our* marriage. Right?"

"Right," Bob said.

"All right. I don't know much about spells," Janice said, rolling up her sleeves, "but I do know machines. Let's get to work."

The next night the ferra visited them at a quarter to eleven. He wore the same white sweater, but he had exchanged his buckskins for tan loafers.

"The king is in a special rush for this," he said. "His newest wife has been pestering the life out of him. It seems that her clothes last for only one washing. Her slaves beat them with rocks."

"Sure," Bob said.

"Help yourself," Janice said.

"That's awfully decent of you," the ferra said gratefully. "I really appreciate it." He picked up a washing machine. "She's waiting now."

He vanished.

Bob offered Janice a cigarette. They sat down on a couch and waited. In half an hour the ferra appeared again.

"What did you do?" he asked.

"Why, what's the matter?" Janice asked sweetly.

"The washer! When the queen started it, it threw out a great cloud of evil-smelling smoke. Then it made some strange noises and stopped."

"In our language," Janice said, blowing a smoke ring, "we would say it was gimmicked."

"Gimmicked?"

"Rigged. Fixed. Strung. And so's everything else in this place."

"But you can't do that!" the ferra said. "It's not playing the game."

"You're so smart," Janice said venomously. "Go ahead and fix it."

"I was boasting," the ferra said in a small voice. "I was much better at sports."

Janice smiled and yawned.

"Well, gee," the ferra said, his little wings twitching nervously.

"Sorry," Bob said.

"This puts me in an awful spot," the ferra said. "I'll be demoted. I'll be thrown out of civil service."

"We can't let ourselves go bankrupt, can we?" Janice asked.

Bob thought for a moment. "Look," he said. "Why *don't* you tell the king you've met a strong countermagic? Tell him he has to pay a tariff to the demons of the underworld if he wants his stuff."

"He won't like it," the ferra said doubtfully.

"Try it anyhow," Bob suggested.

"I'll try," the ferra said, and vanished.

"How much do you think we can charge?" Janice asked.

"Oh, give him standard rates. After all, we've built this store on fair practices. We wouldn't want to discriminate. I still wish I knew where he was from, though."

"He's so rich," Janice said dreamily. "It seems a shame not to—"

"Wait a minute!" Bob shouted. "We can't do it! How can there be refrigerators in two thousand before Christ? Or air conditioners?"

"What do you mean?"

"It would change the whole course of history!" Bob said. "Some smart guy is going to look at those things and figure out how they work. Then the whole course of history will be changed!"

"So what?" Janice asked practically.

"So what? So research will be carried out along different lines. The present will be changed."

"You mean it's impossible?"

"Yes!"

"That's just what I've been saying all along," Janice said triumphantly.

"Oh, stop that," Bob said. "I wish I could figure this out. No matter what country the ferra is from, it's bound to have an effect on the future. We can't have a paradox."

"Why not?" Janice asked, but at that moment the ferra appeared.

"The king has agreed," the ferra said. "Will this pay for what I've taken?" He held out a small sack.

Spilling out the sack, Bob found that it contained about two dozen large rubies, emeralds and diamonds.

"We can't take it," Bob said. "We can't do business with you."

"Don't be superstitious!" Janice shouted, seeing their marriage begin to evaporate again.

"Why not?" the ferra asked.

"We can't introduce modern things into the past," Bob said. "It'll change the present. This world may vanish or something."

"Oh, don't worry about that," the ferra said. "I guarantee nothing will happen."

"But why? I mean, if you introduced a washer in ancient Rome—"

"Unfortunately," the ferra said, "King Alerian's kingdom has no future."

"Would you explain that?"

"Sure." The ferra sat down on the air. "In three years King Alerian and his country will be completely and irrevocably destroyed by forces of nature. Not a person will be saved. Not even a piece of pottery."

"Fine," Janice said, holding a ruby to the light. "We'd better unload while he's still in business."

"I guess that takes care of that," Bob said. Their business was saved, and their marriage was in the immediate future. "How about you?" he asked the ferra.

"Well, I've done rather well on this job," the ferra said. "I think I'll apply for a foreign transfer. I hear there are some wonderful opportunities in Arabian sorcery."

He ran a hand complacently over his blond crewcut. "I'll be seeing you," he said, and started to disappear.

"Just a minute," Bob said. "Would you mind telling me what country you're from? And what country King Alerian is from?"

"Oh, sure," the ferra said, only his head still visible. "I thought you knew. Ferras are the demons of Atlantis."

And he disappeared.

MANNA
PETER PHILLIPS

Peter Phillips is a British journalist of many remarkable skills—he is, for example, the only man I know who can play an ocarina with his left foot tucked behind his head. He is also a splendid science-fiction writer, author of a dozen or so deft and agile stories that have long been cherished by connoisseurs. One of his most celebrated is the delightful Manna, *which is a real literary rarity: a ghost story that's also genuine and legitimate science fiction!*

Take best-quality synthetic protein. Bake it, break it up, steam it, steep it in sucrose, ferment it, add nut oil, piquant spices from the Indies, fruit juices, new flavors from the laboratory, homogenize it, hydrolize it, soak it in brine; pump in glutamic acid, balanced proportions of A, B_1, B_2, C, D, traces of calcium, copper and iron salts, an unadvertised drop of benzedrine; dehydrate, peptonize, irradiate, reheat in malt vapor under pressure, compress, cut into mouth-sized chunks, pack in liquor from an earlier stage of the process—

Miracle Meal.

Everything the Body Needs to Sustain Life and Bounding Vitality, in the Most DEE-LISHUSS Food Ever Devised. It will Invigorate You, Build Muscle, Brain, Nerve. Better than the Banquets of Imperial Rome, Renaissance Italy, Eighteenth-

Century France—all in One Can. The Most Heavenly Taste Thrills You Have Ever Experienced. Gourmets' Dream and Housewives' Delight. You Can Live on It. Eat It for Breakfast, Lunch, Dinner. You'll Never Get Tired of MIRACLE MEAL.

Ad cuts of Zeus contemptuously tossing a bowl of ambrosia over the edge of Mount Olympus and making a goggle-eyed grab for a can of Miracle Meal.

Studio fake-ups of Lucretia Borgia dropping a phial of poison and crying piously: "It Would Be a Sin to Spoil Miracle Meal."

Posters and night-signs of John Doe—or Bill Smith, or Henri Brun, or Hans Schmitt or Wei Lung—balancing precariously on a pyramided pile of empty M.M. cans, eyes closed, mouth pursed in slightly inane ecstasy as he finishes the last mouthful of his hundred-thousandth can.

You could live on it, certainly.

The publicity co-ordinator of the Miracle Meal Corporation chose the victim himself—a young man named Arthur Adelaide from Greenwich Village.

For a year, under the closest medical supervision and observation, Arthur ate nothing but Miracle Meal.

From this Miracle Meal Marathon, as it was tagged by video-print newssheets, he emerged smiling, twice the weight—publicity omitted to mention that he'd been half-starved to begin with—he'd been trying to live off pure art and was a bad artist—perfectly fit, and ten thousand dollars richer.

He was also given a commercial-art job with M.M., designing new labels for the cans.

His abrupt death at the end of an eighty-story drop from his office window a week or two later received little attention.

It would be unreasonable to blame the cumulative effect of M.M., for Arthur was probably a little unbalanced to begin with, whereas M.M. was Perfectly Balanced—a Kitchen in a Can.

Maybe you could get tired of it. But not very quickly. The

flavor was the secret. It was delicious yet strangely and tantalizingly indefinable. It seemed to react progressively on the taste buds so that the taste subtly changed with each mouthful.

One moment it might be *omelette aux fines herbes*, the next, turkey and cranberry, then buckwheat and maple. You'd be through the can before you could make up your mind. So you'd buy another.

Even the can was an improvement on the usual plastic self-heater—shape of a small, shallow pie-dish, with a pre-impressed crystalline fracture in the plastic lid.

Press the inset button on the preheating unit at one side, and when the food was good and hot, a secondary chemical reaction in the unit released a fierce little plunger just inside the perimeter fracture. Slight steam pressure finished the job. The lid flipped off.

Come and get it. You eat right out of the can it comes in. Keep your fingers out, Johnny. Don't you see the hygiplast spoon in its moisture and heat-repellent wrapper fixed under the lid?

The Reverend Malachi Pennyhorse did not eat Miracle Meal. Nor was he impressed when Mr. Stephen Samson, Site Adviser to the Corporation, spoke in large dollar signs of the indirect benefits a factory would bring to the district.

"Why here? You already have one factory in England. Why not extend it?"

"It's our policy, Reverend—"

"Not 'Reverend,' young man. Call me Vicar. Or Mr. Pennyhorse. Or merely Pennyhorse— Go on."

"It's our policy, sir, to keep our factories comparatively small, site them in the countryside for the health of employees, and modify the buildings to harmonize with the prevailing architecture of the district. There is no interference with local amenities. All transport of employees, raw materials, finished product is by silent copter."

Samson laid a triphoto on the vicar's desk. "What would you say that was?"

Mr. Pennyhorse adjusted his pince-nez, looked closely. "Byzantine. Very fine. Around 500 A.D."

"And this—"

"Moorish. Quite typical. Fifteenth century."

Samson said: "They're our factories at Istanbul and Tunis, respectively. At Allahabad, India, we had to put up big notices saying 'This is not a temple or place of worship' because natives kept wandering in and offering up prayers to the processing machines."

Mr. Pennyhorse glanced up quickly. Samson kept his face straight, added: "The report may have been exaggerated, but—you get the idea?"

The vicar said: "I do. What shape do you intend your factory to take in this village?"

"That's why I came to you. The rural district council suggested that you might advise me."

"My inclination, of course, is to advise you to go away and not return."

The vicar looked out of his study window at the sleepy, sun-washed village street, gables of the ancient Corn Exchange, paved marketplace, lichened spire of his own time-kissed church; and, beyond, rolling Wiltshire pastures cradling the peaceful community.

The vicar sighed. "We've held out here so long—I hoped we would remain inviolate in my time, at least. However, I suppose we must consider ourselves fortunate that your corporation has some respect for tradition and the feelings of the . . . uh . . . 'natives.'"

He pulled out a drawer in his desk. "It might help you to understand those feelings if I show you a passage from the very full diary of my predecessor here, who died fifty years ago at the age of ninety-five—we're a long-lived tribe, we clergy. It's an entry he made one hundred years ago—sitting at this very desk."

Stephen Samson took the opened volume.

The century-old handwriting was as readable as typescript.

May 3, 1943. Long, interesting discussion with young American soldier, one of those who are billeted in the village. They term themselves G.I.'s. Told me countryside near his home in Pennsylvania not unlike our Wiltshire downs. Showed him round church. Said he was leaving soon, and added: "I love this place. Nothing like my home town in looks, but the atmosphere's the same—old, and kind of comfortable. And I guess if I came back here a hundred years from now, it wouldn't have changed one bit." An engaging young man. I trust he is right.

Samson looked up. Mr. Pennyhorse said: "That young man may have been one of your ancestors."

Samson gently replaced the old diary on the desk. "He wasn't. My family's Ohioan. But I see what you mean, and respect it. That's why I want you to help us. You will?"

"Do you fish?" asked the vicar, suddenly and irrelevantly.

"Yes, sir. Very fond of the sport."

"Thought so. You're the type. That's why I like you. Take a look at these flies. Seen anything like them? Make 'em myself. One of the finest trout streams in the country just outside the village. Help you? Of course I will."

"Presumption," said Brother James. He eased himself through a gray stone wall by twisting his subexistential plane slightly, and leaned reflectively against a moonbeam that slanted through the branches of an oak.

A second habited and cowled figure materialized beside him. "Perhaps so. But it does my age-wearied heart a strange good to see those familiar walls again casting their shadows over the field."

"A mockery, Brother Gregory. A mere shell that simulates the outlines of our beloved Priory. Think you that even the stones are of that good, gray granite that we built with? Nay! As this cursed simulacrum was a-building, I warped two hands into the solid, laid hold of a massy block, and by the saints, 'twas of such inconsequential weight I might have hurled it skyward with a finger. And within, is there aught which we may recognize? No chapel, no cloisters, no refectory—only long, geometrical rooms. And what devilries and unholy rites may not be centered about those strange mechanisms with which the rooms are filled?"

At the tirade, Brother Gregory sighed and thrust back his cowl to let the gracious moonbeams play on his tonsured head. "For an Untranslated One of some thousand years' standing," he said, "you exhibit a mulish ignorance, Brother James. You would deny men all advancement. I remember well your curses when first we saw horseless carriages and flying machines."

"Idols!" James snapped. "Men worship them. Therefore are they evil."

"You are so good, Brother James," Gregory said, with the heaviest sarcasm. "So good, it is my constant wonderment that you have had to wait so long for Translation Upwards. Do you think that Dom Pennyhorse, the present incumbent of Selcor—a worthy man, with reverence for the past—would permit evil rites within his parish? You are a befuddled old anachronism, brother."

"That," said James, "is quite beyond sufferance. For you to speak thus of Translation, when it was your own self-indulgent pursuit of carnal pleasures that caused us to be bound here through the centuries!"

Brother Gregory said coldly: "It was not I who inveigled the daughter of Ronald the Wry-Neck into the kitchen garden, thus exposing the weak flesh of a brother to grievous temptation."

There was silence for a while save for the whisper of a midnight breeze through the branches of the oak, and the muted call of a nightbird from the far woods.

Gregory extended a tentative hand and lightly touched the sleeve of James's habit. "The argument might proceed for yet another century and bring us no nearer translation. Besides, it is not such unbearable penance, my brother. Were we not both lovers of the earth, of this fair countryside?"

James shrugged. Another silence. Then he fingered his gaunt

white cheeks. "What shall we do, Brother Gregory? Shall we—appear to them?"

Gregory said: "I doubt whether common warp manifestation would be efficacious. As dusk fell tonight, I overheard a conversation between Dom Pennyhorse and a tall, young-featured man who has been concerned in the building of this simulacrum. The latter spoke in one of the dialects of the Americas; and it was mentioned that several of the men who will superintend the working of the machines within will also be from the United States—for a time at least. It is not prudent to haunt Americans in the normal fashion. Their attitude towards such matters is notoriously—unseemly."

"We could polter," suggested Brother James.

Gregory replaced his cowl. "Let us review the possibilities, then," he said, "remembering that our subetheric energy is limited."

They walked slowly together over the meadow towards the resuscitated gray walls of Selcor Priory. Blades of grass, positively charged by their passage, sprang suddenly upright, relaxed slowly into limpness as the charge leaked away.

They halted at the walls to adjust their planes of incidence and degree of tenuity, then passed inside.

The new Miracle Meal machines had had their first test run. The bearings on the dehydrator pumps were still warm as two black figures, who seemed to carry with them an air of vast and wistful loneliness, paced silently between rows of upright cylinders which shone dully in moonlight diffused through narrow windows.

"Here," said Gregory, the taller of the two, softly, "did we once walk the cloisters in evening meditation."

Brother James's broad features showed signs of unease. He felt more than mere nostalgia.

"Power—what are they using? Something upsets my bones. I am queasy, as when a thunderstorm is about to break. Yet there is no static."

Gregory stopped, looked at his hand. There was a faint blue aura at his fingertips. "Slight neutron escape," he said. "They have a small thorium-into-233 pile somewhere. It needs better shielding."

"You speak riddles."

Gregory said, with a little impatience: "You have the entire science section of the village library at your disposal at nightfall for the effort of a trifling polter, yet for centuries you have read nothing but the *Lives of the Saints*. So, of course, I speak riddles—to you. You are even content to remain in ignorance of the basic principles of your own structure and functioning, doing everything by traditional thought-rote and rule of thumb. But I am not so content; and of my knowledge, I can assure you that the radiation will not harm you unless you warp to solid and sit atop the pile when it is in full operation." Gregory smiled. "And then, dear brother, you would doubtless be so uncomfortable that you would dewarp before any harm could be done beyond the loss of a little energy that would be replaced in time. Let us proceed."

They went through three departments before Brother Gregory divined the integrated purpose of the vats, driers, conveyor-tubes, belts and containers.

"The end product, I'm sure, is a food of sorts," he said, "and by some quirk of fate, it is stored in approximately the position that was once occupied by our kitchen store—if my sense of orientation has not been bemused by these strange internal surroundings."

The test run of the assembly had produced a few score cans of Miracle Meal. They were stacked on metal shelves which would tilt and gravity-feed them into the shaft leading up to the crating machine. Crated, they would go from there to the copter-loading bay on the roof.

Brother James reached out to pick up a loose can. His hand went through it twice.

"Polt, you dolt!" said Brother Gregory. "Or are you trying to be miserly with your confounded energy? Here, let me do it."

The telekineticized can sprang into his solid hands. He turned it about, slightly increasing his infrared receptivity to read the label, since the storeroom was in darkness.

"Miracle Meal. Press Here."

He pressed, pressed again, and was closely examining the can when, after thirty seconds, the lid flipped off, narrowly missing his chin.

Born, and living, in more enlightened times, Brother Gregory's inquiring mind and insatiable appetite for facts would have made him a research worker. He did not drop the can. His hands were quite steady. He chuckled. He said: "Ingenious, very ingenious. See—the food is hot."

He warped his nose and back-palate into solid and delicately inhaled vapors. His eyes widened. He frowned, inhaled again. A beatific smile spread over his thin face.

"Brother James—warp your nose!"

The injunction, in other circumstances, might have been considered both impolite and unnecessary. Brother James was no beauty, and his big, blunt, snoutlike nose, which had been a flaring red in life, was the least prepossessing of his features.

But he warped it, and sniffed.

M. M. SALES LEAFLET NUMBER 14: It Will Sell By Its Smell Alone.

Gregory said hesistantly: "Do you think, Brother James, that we might—"

James licked his lips, from side to side, slowly. "It would surely take a day's accumulation of energy to hold digestive and alimentary in solid for a sufficient period. But—"

"Don't be a miser," said Gregory. "There's a spoon beneath the lid. Get a can for yourself. And don't bother with digestive. Teeth, palate and throat are sufficient. It would not digest in any case. It remains virtually unchanged. But going down—ah, bliss!"

It went down. Two cans.

"Do you remember, brother," said James, in a weak, reminiscing voice, "what joy it was to eat and be strengthened. And now to eat is to be weakened."

Brother Gregory's voice was faint but happy. "Had there been food of this character available before our First Translation, I doubt whether other desires of the flesh would have appealed to me. But what was our daily fare set on the refectory table: peas; lentils; cabbage soup; hard, tasteless cheese. Year after year—*ugh!*"

"Health-giving foods," murmured Brother James, striving to be righteous even in his exhaustion. "Remember when we bribed the kitchener to get extra portions. Good trenchermen, we. Had we not died of the plague before our Priory became rich and powerful, then, by the Faith, our present bodies would be of greater girth."

"Forms, not bodies," said Gregory, insisting even in *his* exhaustion on scientific exactitudes. "Variable fields, consisting of open lattices of energy foci resolvable into charged particles—and thus solid matter—when they absorb energy beyond a certain stage. In other words, my dear ignorant brother, when we polt. The foci themselves—or rather the spaces between them—act as a limited-capacity storage battery for the slow accretion of this energy from cosmic sources, which may be controlled and concentrated in the foci by certain thought-patterns."

Talking was an increasing effort in his energy-low state.

"When we polt," he went on slowly, "we take up heat, air cools, live people get cold shivers; de-polt, give up heat, live people get clammy, cold-hot feeling; set up 'lectrostatic field, live people's hair stan's on end"—his voice was trailing into deep, blurred inaudibility, like a mechanical phonograph running down, but James wasn't listening anyway—"an' then when we get Translated Up'ards by The Power that Is, all the energy goes back where it came from an' we jus' become thought. T h a s s a l l. Thought. Thought, t h o u g h t, thought, thought . . ."

The phonograph ran down, stopped. There was silence in the transit storeroom of the Selcor Priory Factory branch of the Miracle Meal Corporation.

For a while.

Then—

"THOUGHT!"

The shout brought Brother James from his uneasy, uncontrolled repose at the nadir of an energy balance.

"What is it?" he grumbled. "I'm too weak to listen to any of your theorizing."

"Theorizing! I have it!"

"Conserve your energies, brother, else will you be too weak even to twist yourself from this place."

Both monks had permitted their forms to relax into a corner of the storeroom, supine, replete in disrepletion.

Brother Gregory sat up with an effort.

"Listen, you attenuated conserve of very nothingness, I have a way to thwart, bemuse, mystify and irritate these crass philistines—and nothing so simple that a psychic investigator could put a thumb on us. What are we, Brother James?"

It was a rhetorical question, and Brother James had barely formulated his brief reply—"Ghosts"—before Brother Gregory, energized in a way beyond his own understanding by his own enthusiasm, went on: "Fields, in effect. Mere lines of force, in our un-polted state. What happens if we whirl? A star whirls. It has mass, rate of angular rotation, degree of compactness—therefore, gravity. Why? Because it has a field to start with. But we are our own fields. We need neither mass nor an excessive rate of rotation to achieve the same effect. Last week I grounded a high-flying wood pigeon by whirling. It shot down to me through the air, and I'd have been buffeted by its pinions had I not stood aside. It hit the ground—not too heavily, by the grace of Saint Barbara—recovered and flew away."

The great nose of Brother James glowed pinkly for a moment.

"You fuddle and further weaken me by your prating. Get to your point, if you have such. And explain how we may do anything in our present unenergized state, beyond removing ourselves to a nexus point for recuperation."

Brother Gregory warped his own nose into solid in order to scratch its tip. He felt the need of this reversion to a life habit, which had once aided him in marshaling his thoughts.

"You think only of personal energy," he said scornfully. "We don't need that, to whirl. It is an accumulative process, yet we gain nothing, lose nothing. Matter is not the only thing we can warp. If you will only listen, you woof of unregenerate and forgotten flesh, I will try to explain without mathematics."

He talked.

After a while, Brother James's puzzled frown gave way to a faint smile. "Perhaps I understand," he said.

"Then forgive me for implying you were a moron," said Gregory. "Stand up, Brother James."

Calls on transatlantic tight-beam cost heavy. Anson Dewberry, Miracle Meal Overseas Division head, pointed this out to Mr. Stephen Samson three times during their conversation.

"Listen," said Samson at last, desperately, "I'll take no more delegation of authority. In my contract, it says I'm site adviser. That means I'm architect and negotiator, not detective or scientist or occultist. I offered to stay on here to supervise building because I happen to like the place. I like the pubs. I like the people. I like the fishing. But it wasn't in my contract. And I'm now standing on that contract. Building is finished to schedule, plant installed—your tech men, incidentally, jetted out of here without waiting to catch snags after the first runoff—and now I'm through. The machines are running, the cans are coming off—and if the copters don't collect, that's for you and the London office to bat your brains out over. And the Lord forgive that mess of terminal prepositions," he added in lower voice. Samson was a purist in the matter of grammar.

Anson Dewberry jerked his chair nearer the scanner in his New York office. His pink, round face loomed in Samson's screen like that of an avenging cherub.

"Don't you have no gendarmes around that place?" Mr. Dewberry was no purist, in moments of stress. "Get guards on, hire some militia, check employees. Ten thousand cans of M.M. don't just evaporate."

"They do," Samson replied sadly. "Maybe it's the climate. And for the seventh time, I tell you I've done all that. I've had men packed so tightly around the place that even an orphan neutron couldn't get by. This morning I had two men from Scotland Yard gumming around. They looked at the machines, followed the assembly through to the transit storeroom, examined the electrolocks and mauled their toe-caps trying to boot a dent in the door. Then the top one—that is, the one who only looked half-asleep—said, 'Mr. Samson, sir, do you think it's . . . uh . . . possible . . . that . . . uh . . . this machine of yours . . . uh . . . goes into reverse when your . . . uh . . . backs are turned and . . . uh . . . sucks the cans back again?' "

Grating noises that might have been an incipient death rattle slid over the tight-beam from New York.

Samson nodded, a smirk of mock sympathy on his tanned, humor-wrinkled young face.

The noises ended with a gulp. The image of Dewberry thrust up a hesitant forefinger in interrogation. "Hey! Maybe there's something to that, at that—would it be possible?"

Samson groaned a little. "I wouldn't really know or overmuch care. But I have doubts. Meantime—"

"Right." Dewberry receded on the screen. "I'll jet a man over tonight. The best. From Research. Full powers. Hand over to him. Take some of your vacation. Design some more blamed mosques or tabernacles. Go fishing."

"A sensible suggestion," Samson said. "Just what I was about to do. It's a glorious afternoon here, sun a little misted, grass green, stream flowing cool and deep, fish lazing in the pools where the willow-shadows fall—"

The screen blanked. Dewberry was no purist, and no poet either.

Samson made a school-kid face. He switched off the fluor lamps that supplemented the illumination from a narrow window in the supervisor's office—which, after studying the ground-plan of the original Selcor Priory, he had sited in the space that was occupied centuries before by the business sanctum of the Prior—got up from his desk and walked through a Norman archway into the sunlight.

He breathed the meadow-sweet air deeply, with appreciation.

The Reverend Malachi Pennyhorse was squatting with loose-jointed ease against the wall. Two fishing rods in brown canvas covers lay across his lap. He was studying one of the trout-flies nicked into the band of his ancient hat. His balding, brown pate was bared to the sun. He looked up.

"What fortune, my dear Stephen?"

"I convinced him at last. He's jetting a man over tonight. He told me to go fishing."

"Injunction unnecessary, I should imagine. Let's go. We shan't touch a trout with the sky as clear as this, but I have some float tackle for lazier sport." They set off across a field. "Are you running the plant today?"

Samson nodded his head towards a faint hum. "Quarter-speed. That will give one copter-load for the seventeen-hundred-hours collection, and leave enough over to go in the transit store for the night and provide Newberry's man with some data. Or rather, lack of it."

"Where do you think it's going?"

"I've given up guessing."

Mr. Pennyhorse paused astride a stile and looked back at the gray bulk of the Priory. "I could guess who's responsible," he said, and chuckled.

"Uh? Who?"

Mr. Pennyhorse shook his head. "Leave that to your investigator."

A few moments later he murmured as if to himself: "What a haunt! Ingenious devils."

But when Stephen Samson looked at him inquiringly, he added: "But I can't guess where your cans have been put."

And he would say nothing more on the subject.

Who would deny that the pure of heart are often simple-minded? (The obverse of the proposition need not be argued.) And that cause-effect relations are sometimes divined more readily by the intuition of simpletons than the logic of scholars?

Brother Simon Simplex—Simple Simon to later legends—looked open-mouthed at the array of strange objects on the stone shelves of the kitchen storeroom. He was not surprised—his mouth was always open, even in sleep.

He took down one of the objects and examined it with mild curiosity. He shook it, turned it around, thrust a forefinger into a small depression. Something gave slightly, but there was no other aperture. He replaced it on the shelf.

When his fellow-kitchener returned, he would ask him the purpose of the objects—if he could remember to do so. Simon's memory was poor. Each time the rota brought him onto kitchen duty for a week, he had to be instructed afresh in the business of serving meals in the refectory: platter so, napkin thus, spoon here, finger bowls half-filled, three water pitchers, one before the Prior, one in the center, one at the foot of the table— "and when you serve, tread softly and do not breathe down the necks of the brothers."

Even now could he hear the slight scrape of benches on stone as the monks, with bowed heads, freshly washed hands in the sleeves of their habits, filed slowly into the refectory and took their seats at the long oak table. And still his fellow-kitchener had not returned from the errand. Food was prepared—dared he begin to serve alone?

It was a great problem for Simon, brother in the small House of Selcor, otherwise Selcor Priory, poor cell-relation to the rich monastery of the Cluniac Order at Battle, in the year 1139 A.D.

Steam pressure in the triggered can of Miracle Meal did its work. The lid flipped. The aroma issued.

Simon's mouth nearly shut as he sniffed.

The calm and unquestioning acceptance of the impossible is another concomitant of simplicity and purity of heart. To the good and simple Simon the rising of the sun each morning and the singing of birds were recurrent miracles. Compared with these, a laboratory miracle of the year 2043 A.D. was as nothing.

Here was a new style of platter, filled with hot food, ready to serve. Wiser minds than his had undoubtedly arranged matters. His fellow-kitchener, knowing the task was thus simplified, had left him to serve alone.

He had merely to remove the covers from these platters and carry them into the refectory. To remove the covers—cause—effect—the intuition of a simple mind.

Simon carried fourteen of the platters to the kitchen table, pressed buttons and waited.

He was gravely tempted to sample the food himself, but all-inclusive Benedictine rules forbade kitcheners to eat until their brothers had been served.

He carried a loaded tray into the refectory where the monks sat in patient silence except for the lone voice of the Reader, who stood at a raised lectern and intoned from the *Lives of the Saints*.

Pride that he had been thought fit to carry out the duty alone made Simon less clumsy than usual. He served the Prior, Dom Holland, first, almost deftly; then the other brothers, in two trips to the kitchen.

A spicy, rich, titillating fragrance filled the refectory. The intoning of the *Lives of the Saints* faltered for a moment as the mouth of the Reader filled with saliva, then he grimly continued.

At Dom Holland's signal, the monks ate.

The Prior spooned the last drops of gravy into his mouth. He sat back. A murmur arose. He raised a hand. The monks quietened. The Reader closed his book.

Dom Holland was a man of faith; but he did not accept miracles or even the smallest departures from routine existence without questioning. He had sternly debated with himself whether he should question the new platters and the new food before or after eating. The aroma decided him. He ate first.

Now he got up, beckoned to a senior monk to follow him, and paced with unhurried calmness to the kitchen.

Simon had succumbed. He was halfway through his second tin.

He stood up, locking his fingers.

"Whence comes this food, my son?" asked Dom Holland, in sonorous Latin.

Simon's mouth opened wider. His knowledge of the tongue was confined to prayers.

Impatiently the Prior repeated the question in the English dialect of the district.

Simon pointed, and led them to the storeroom.

"I looked, and it was here," he said simply. The words were to become famed.

His fellow-kitchener was sought—he was found dozing in a warm corner of the kitchen garden—and questioned. He shook his head. The provisioner rather reluctantly disclaimed credit.

Dom Holland thought deeply, then gave instructions for a general assembly. The plastic "platters" and the hygiplast spoons were carefully examined. There were murmurs of wonderment at the workmanship. The discussion lasted two hours.

Simon's only contribution was to repeat with pathetic insistence: "I looked and it was there."

He realized dimly that he had become a person of some importance.

His face became a mask of puzzlement when the Prior summed up:

"Our simple but blessed brother, Simon Simplex, it seems to me, has become an instrument or vessel of some thaumaturgical manifestation. It would be wise, however, to await further demonstration before the matter is referred to higher authorities."

The storeroom was sealed and two monks were deputed as nightguards.

Even with the possibility of a miracle on his hands, Dom Holland was not prepared to abrogate the Benedictine rule of only one main meal a day. The storeroom wasn't opened until early afternoon of the following day.

It was opened by Simon, in the presence of the Prior, a scribe, the provisioner, and two senior monks.

Released, a pile of Miracle Meal cans toppled forward like a crumbling cliff, slithering and clattering in noisy profusion around Simon's legs, sliding over the floor of the kitchen.

Simon didn't move. He was either too surprised or cunningly aware of the effectiveness of the scene. He stood calf-deep in cans, pointed at the jumbled stack inside the storeroom, sloping up nearly to the stone roof, and said his little piece:

"I look, and it is here."

"Kneel, my sons," said Dom Holland gravely, and knelt.

Manna.

And at a time when the Priory was hard-pressed to maintain even its own low standard of subsistence, without helping the scores of dispossessed refugees encamped in wattle shacks near its protecting walls.

The countryside was scourged by a combination of civil and foreign war. Stephen of Normandy against Matilda of Anjou for the British throne. They could not control their own followers. When the Flemish mercenaries of King Stephen were not chasing Queen Matilda's Angevins back over the borders of Wiltshire, they were plundering the lands and possession of nominal supporters of Stephen. The Angevins and the barons who supported Matilda's cause quite impartially did the same, then pillaged each other's property, castle against castle, baron against baron.

It was anarchy and free-for-all—but nothing for the ignored serfs, bondmen, villeins and general peasantry, who fled from stricken homes and roamed the countryside in bands of starving thousands. Some built shacks in the inviolate shadow of churches and monasteries.

Selcor Priory had its quota of barefoot, raggedy men, women and children—twelfth-century Displaced Persons.

They were a headache to the Prior, kindly Dom Holland—until Simple Simon's Miracle.

There were seventy recipients of the first handout of Miracle Meal cans from the small door in the Priory's walled kitchen garden.

The next day there were three hundred, and the day after that, four thousand. Good news doesn't need radio to get around fast.

Fourteen monks worked eight-hour shifts for twenty-four hours, hauling stocks from the capacious storeroom, pressing buttons, handing out steaming platters to orderly lines of refugees.

Two monks, shifting the last few cans from the store, were suddenly buried almost to their necks by the arrival of a fresh consignment, which piled up out of thin air.

Providence, it seemed, did not depend solely upon the intervention of Simon Simplex. The Priory itself and all its inhabitants were evidently blessed.

The Abbot of Battle, Dom Holland's superior, a man of great girth and great learning, visited the Priory. He confirmed the miracle—by studying the label on the can.

After several hours' work in the Prior's office, he announced to Holland:

"The script presented the greatest difficulty. It is an extreme simplification of letter-forms at present in use by Anglo-Saxon scholars. The pertinent text is a corruption—if I may be pardoned the use of such a term in the circumstances—of the Latin '*miraculum*' compounded with the word '*maél*' from our own barbarous tongue—so, clearly, Miracle Meal!"

Dom Holland murmured his awe of this learning.

The Abbot added, half to himself: "Although why the nature of the manifestation should be thus advertised in repetitive engraving, when it is self-evident . . ." He shrugged. "The ways of Providence are passing strange."

Brother Gregory, reclining in the starlight near his favorite oak, said:

"My only regret is that we cannot see the effect of our gift— the theoretical impact of a modern product—usually a weapon—on past ages is a well-tried topic of discussion and speculation among historians, scientists, economists and writers of fantasy."

Brother James, hunched in vague adumbration on a wall behind, said: "You are none of those things, else might you explain why it is that, if these cans have reached the period for which, according to your abstruse calculations, they were destined—an age in which we were both alive—we cannot remember such an event, or why it is not recorded in histories of the period."

"It was a time of anarchy, dear brother. Many records were destroyed. And as for our memories—well, great paradoxes of time are involved. One might as profitably ask how many angels may dance on the point of a pin. Now if you should wish to know how many atoms might be accommodated in a like position . . ."

Brother Gregory was adroit at changing the subject. He didn't wish to speculate aloud until he'd figured out all the paradox possibilities. He'd already discarded an infinity of time-streams as intellectually unsatisfying, and was toying with the concept of recurrent worlds. . . .

"Dom Pennyhorse has guessed that it is our doing."

"What's that?"

Brother James repeated the information smugly.

Gregory said slowly: "Well, he is not—unsympathetic—to us."

"Assuredly, brother, we have naught to fear from him, nor from the pleasant young man with whom he goes fishing. But this young man was today in consultation with his superior, and an investigator is being sent from America."

"Psychic investigator, eh? Phooey. We'll tie him in knots," said Gregory complacently.

"I assume," said Brother James, with a touch of self-righteousness, "that these vulgar colloquialisms to which you sometimes have recourse are another result of your nocturnal reading. They offend my ear. 'Phooey,' indeed—No, this investigator is one with whom you will undoubtedly find an affinity. I gather that he is from a laboratory—a scientist of sorts."

Brother Gregory sat up and rubbed his tonsure thoughtfully. "That," he admitted, "is different." There was a curious mixture of alarm and eagerness in his voice. "There are means of detecting the field we employ."

An elementary electroscope was one of the means. An ionization indicator and a thermometer were others. They were all bolted firmly on a bench just inside the storeroom. Wires led from them under the door to a jury-rigged panel outside.

Sandy-haired Sidney Meredith of M. M. Research sat in front of the panel on a folding stool, watching dials with intense blue eyes, chin propped in hands.

Guards had been cleared from the factory. He was alone, on the advice of Mr. Pennyhorse, who had told him: "If, as I suspect, it's the work of two of my . . . uh . . . flock . . . two very ancient parishioners . . . they are more likely to play their tricks in the absence of a crowd."

"I get it," Meredith had said. "Should be interesting."

It was.

He poured coffee from a thermos without taking his eyes from the panel. The thermometer reading was dropping slowly.

Ionization was rising. From inside the store came the faint rasp of moving objects.

Meredith smiled, sighted a thumb-size camera, recorded the panel readings. "This," he said softly, "will make a top feature in the *Journal*: "The most intensive psychic and poltergeist phenomena ever recorded. M.M.'s top tech troubleshooter spikes spooks.' "

There was a faint snap beyond the door. Dials swooped back to zero. Meredith quit smiling and daydreaming.

"Hey—play fair!" he called.

The whisper of a laugh answered him, and a soft, hollow whine, as of a wind cycloning into outer space.

He grabbed the door, pulled. It resisted. It was like trying to break a vacuum. He knelt, lit a cigarette, held it near the bottom of the nearly flush-fitting door. A thin streamer of smoke curled down and was drawn swiftly through the barely perceptible crack.

The soft whine continued for a few seconds, began to die away.

Meredith yanked at the door again. It gave, to a slight ingush of air. He thrust his foot in the opening, said calmly into the empty blackness: "When you fellers have quite finished—I'm coming in. Don't go away. Let's talk."

He slipped inside, closed the door, stood silent for a moment. He sniffed. Ozone. His scalp prickled. He scratched his head, felt the hairs standing upright. And it was cold.

He said: "Right. No point in playing dumb or covering up, boys." He felt curiously ashamed of the platitudes as he uttered them. "I must apologize for breaking in," he added—and meant it. "But this has got to finish. And if you're not willing to—cooperate—I think I know now how to finish it."

Another whisper of a laugh. And two words, faint, gently mocking: "Do you?"

Meredith strained his eyes against the darkness. He saw only the nerve-patterns in his own eyes. He shrugged.

"If you won't play—" He switched on a blaze of fluor lamps.

The long steel shelves were empty. There was only one can of Miracle Meal left in the store.

He felt it before he saw it. It dropped on his head, clattered to the plastocrete floor. When he'd retrieved his breath, he kicked it savagely to the far end of the store and turned to his instruments.

The main input lead had been pulled away. The terminal had been loosened first.

He unclamped a wide-angle infrared camera, waited impatiently for the developrinter to act, pulled out the print.

And laughed. It wasn't good line-caricature of himself, but it was recognizable, chiefly by the shock of unruly hair.

The lines were slightly blurred, as though written by a needle-point of light directly on the film. There was a jumble of writing over and under it.

"Old English, I suppose," he murmured. He looked closer. The writing above the caricature was a de Sitter version of the Riemann-Christoffel tensor, followed in crabbed but readable modern English by the words: "Why reverse the sign? Do we act like anti-particles?"

Underneath the drawing was an energy tensor and a comment: "You will notice that magnetic momenta contribute a negative density and pressure."

A string of symbols followed, ending with an equals sign and a query mark. And another comment: "You'll need to take time out to balance this one."

Meredith read the symbols, then sat down heavily on the edge of the instrument bench and groaned. Time *out*. But Time was already out, and there was neither matter nor radiation in a de Sitter universe.

Unless—

He pulled out a notebook, started to scribble.

An hour later Mr. Pennyhorse and Stephen Samson came in.

Mr. Pennyhorse said: "My dear young fellow, we were quite concerned. We thought—"

He stopped. Meredith's blue eyes were slightly out of focus. There were beads of sweat on his brow despite the coolness of the storeroom. Leaves from his notebook and cigarette stubs littered the floor around his feet.

He jumped like a pricked frog when the vicar gently tapped his shoulder, and uttered a vehement cuss-word that startled even the broad-minded cleric.

Samson tutted.

Meredith muttered: "Sorry, sir. But I think I nearly had it."

"What, my son?"

Meredith looked like a ruffle-haired schoolboy. His eyes came back into focus. "A crossword-puzzle clue," he said. "Set by a spook with a super-I.Q. Two quite irreconcilable systems of mathematics lumped together, the signs in an extended energy tensor reversed, merry hell played with a temporal factor—and yet it was beginning to make sense."

He smiled wryly. "A ghost who unscrews terminals before he breaks connections and who can make my brain boil is a ghost worth meeting."

Mr. Pennyhorse eased his pince-nez. "Uh . . . yes. Now, don't you think it's time you came to bed? It's four A.M. My housekeeper has made up a comfortable place on the divan in the sitting room." He took Meredith's arm and steered him from the store.

As they walked across the dewy meadows towards the vicarage, with the first pale streaks of dawn showing in the sky, Samson said: "How about the cans?"

"Time," replied Meredith vaguely, "will tell."

"And the guards?"

"Pay them off. Send them away. Keep the plant rolling. Fill the transit store tonight. And I want a freighter copter to take me to London University this afternoon."

Back in the transit store, the discarded leaves from Meredith's notebook fluttered gently upwards in the still air and disappeared.

Brother James said: "He is alone again."

They looked down on the sandy head of Sidney Meredith from the vantage point of a dehydrating tower.

"So I perceive. And I fear this may be our last uh . . . consignment to our erstwhile brothers," said Gregory thoughtfully.

"Why?"

"You will see. In giving him the clue to what we were doing, I gave him the clue to what we are, essentially."

They drifted down towards the transit store.

"After you, Brother James," said Brother Gregory with excessive politeness.

James adjusted his plane of incidence, started through the wall, and—

Shot backwards with a voiceless scream of agony.

Brother Gregory laughed. "I'm sorry. But that's why it will be our last consignment. Heterodyning is painful. He is a very intelligent fellow. The next time, he will take care to screen both his ultra-short generator and controls so that I cannot touch them."

Brother James recovered. "You . . . you use me as a confounded guinea pig! By the saints, you appear to have more sympathy with the man than with me!"

"Not more sympathy, my beloved brother, but certainly much more in common," Brother Gregory replied frankly. "Wait."

He drifted behind Meredith's back and poltered the tip of one finger to flick a lightly soldered wire from a terminal behind a switch. Meredith felt his scalp tingle. A pilot light on his panel blinked out.

Meredith got up from his stool, stretched lazily, grinned into the empty air. He said aloud: "Right. Help yourselves. But I warn you—once you're in, you don't come out until you agree to talk. I have a duplicate set and a built-in circuit-tester. The only way you can spike them is by busting tubes. And I've a hunch you wouldn't do that."

"No," James muttered. "You wouldn't. Let us go."

"No," Gregory answered. "Inside quickly—and whirl. Afterwards, I shall speak with him. He is a youth of acute sensibilities and gentleness, whose word is his bond."

Gregory urged his fellow-monk to the wall. They passed within.

Meredith heard nothing, until a faint whine began in the store. He waited until it died away, then knocked on the door. It seemed, crazily, the correct thing to do.

He went into the darkness. "You there?"

A low and pleasant voice, directionless: "Yes. Why didn't you switch on your duplicate generator?"

Meredith breathed deep. "I didn't think it would be necessary. I feel we understand each other. My name is Sidney Meredith."

"Mine is Gregory of Ramsbury."

"And your—friend?"

"James Brasenose. I may say that he disapproves highly of this conversation."

"I can understand that. It is unusual. But then, you're a very unusual . . . um—"

" 'Ghost' is the common term, Mr. Meredith. Rather inadequate, I think, for supranormal phenomena which are, nevertheless, subject to known laws. Most Untranslated spirits remain quite ignorant of their own powers before final Translation. It was only by intensive reading and thought that I determined the principles and potentialities of my construction."

"Anti-particles?"

"According to de Sitter," said Brother Gregory, "that is what we should be. But we are not mere mathematical expressions. I prefer the term 'energy foci.' From a perusal of the notes you left behind yesterday morning—and, of course, from your use of ultra-short waves tonight—it seems you struck the correct train of deduction immediately. Incidentally, where did you obtain the apparatus at such short notice?"

"London University."

Brother Gregory sighed. "I should like to visit their laboratories. But we are bound to this area by a form of moral compulsion that I cannot define or overcome. Only vicariously, through the achievements of others, may I experience the thrill of research."

"You don't do so badly," Meredith said. He was mildly surprised that he felt quite so sane and at ease, except for the darkness. "Would you mind if we had a light?"

"I must be semipolted—or warped—to speak with you. It's not a pleasant sight—floating lungs, larynx, palate, tongue and lips. I'd feel uncomfortable for you. We might appear for you later, if you wish."

"Right. But keep talking. Give me the how and the why. I want this for my professional journal."

"Will you see that the issue containing your paper is placed in the local history?"

"Surely," Meredith said. "Two copies."

"Brother James is not interested. Brother James, will you kindly stop whispering nonsense and remove yourself to a nexus point for a while? I intend to converse with Mr. Meredith. Thank you."

The voice of Brother Gregory came nearer, took on a slightly professorial tone. "Any massive and rotating body assumes the qualities of magnetism—or rather, gravitic, one-way flux—by virtue of its rotation, and the two quantities of magnetic momentum and angular momentum are always proportional to one another, as you doubtless know."

Meredith smiled inwardly. A lecture on elementary physics from a ghost. Well—maybe not so elementary. He remembered the figures that he'd sweated over. But he could almost envisage the voice of Brother Gregory emanating from a black-gowned instructor in front of a classroom board.

"Take a star," the voice continued. "Say 78 Virginis —from whose flaming promontories the effect was first deduced a hundred years ago—and put her against a counter-whirling star of similar mass. What happens? Energy warp, of the kind we use every time we polt. But something else happens—did you infer it from my incomplete expression?"

Meredith grinned. He said: "Yes. Temporal warp."

"Oh." There was a trace of disappointment in the voice.

Meredith added quickly: "But it certainly gave me a headache figuring it out."

Gregory was evidently mollified by the admission. "Solids through time," he went on. "Some weeks ago, calculating that my inherent field was as great in certain respects as that of 78 Virginis, I whirled against a longitudinal line, and forced a stone back a few days—the nearest I could get to laboratory confirmation. Knowing there would be a logical extension of the effect if I whirled against a field as strong as my own, I persuaded Brother James to cooperate with me—and you know the result."

"How far back?"

"According to my mathematics, the twelfth century, at a time when we were—alive. I would appreciate your views on the paradoxes involved."

Meredith said: "Certainly. Let's go over your math together first. If it fits in with what I've already figured, perhaps I'll have a suggestion to make. You appreciate, of course, that I can't let you have any more cans?"

"Quite. I must congratulate your company on manufacturing a most delicious comestible. If you will hand me the roll of infrared film from your camera, I can make my calculations visible to you on the emulsion in the darkness. Thank you. It is a pity," Gregory murmured, "that we could not see with our own eyes what disposal they made of your product in the days of our Priory."

When, on the morning of a certain bright summer day in 1139, the daily consignment of Miracle Meal failed to arrive at Selcor Priory, thousands of disappointed refugees went hungry.

The Prior, Dom Holland—who, fortunately for his sanity or

at least his peace of mind, was not in a position to separate cause from effect—attributed the failure of supply to the lamentable departure from grace and moral standards of two of the monks.

By disgracing themselves in the kitchen garden with a female refugee, he said, they had obviously rendered the Priory unfit to receive any further miraculous bounty.

The abject monks, Brother Gregory and Brother James, were severely chastised and warned in drastic theological terms that it would probably be many centuries before they had sufficiently expiated their sins to attain blessedness.

On the morning of another bright summer day, the Reverend Malachi Pennyhorse and Stephen Samson were waiting for Sidney Meredith in the vicar's comfortable study.

Meredith came in, sank into a century-old leather easy chair, stretched his shoes, damp with dew from the meadow grass, towards the flames. He accepted a glass of whiskey gratefully, sipped it.

He said: "The cans are there. And from now on, they stay in the transit store, until the copters collect."

There was an odd note of regret in his voice.

Samson said: "Fine. Now maybe you'll tell us what happened yesterday."

Mr. Pennyhorse said: "You . . . uh . . . liked my parishioners, then?"

Meredith combined a smile and a sigh. "I surely did. That Brother Gregory had the most intense and dispassionate intellectual curiosity of anyone I ever met. He nearly grounded me on some aspects of energy mathematics. I could have used him in my department. He'd have made a great research man. Brother James wasn't a bad old guy, either. They appeared for me—"

"How did you get rid of them?" Samson interrupted.

"They got rid of themselves. Gregory told me how, by whirling against each other with gravitic fields cutting, they drew the cans into a vortex of negated time that threw them way back to the twelfth century. After we'd been through his math, I suggested they whirl together."

"What—and throw the cans ahead?"

"No. Themselves, in a sense, since they precipitated a future, hoped-for state. Gregory had an idea what would happen. So did I. He'd only discovered the effect recently. Curiosity got the better of him. He had to try it out straight away. They whirled together. The fields reinforced, instead of negated. Enough in-going energy was generated to whoop their own charges well above capacity and equilibrium. They just—went. As Gregory would put it—they were Translated."

"Upwards, I trust," said Mr. Pennyhorse gently.

"Amen to that," said Samson.

Upwards—

Pure thought, unbound, Earth-rid, roaming free amid the wild bright stars—

Thought to Thought, over galactic vastnesses, wordless, yet swift and clear, before egos faded—

"Why didn't I think of this before? We might have Translated ourselves centuries ago."

"But then we would never have tasted Miracle Meal."

"That is a consideration," agreed the Thought that had been Brother Gregory.

"Remember our third can?" came the Thought that had been Brother James.

But there was no reply. Something of far greater urgency and interest than memories of Miracle Meal had occurred to the Thought that had been Brother Gregory.

With eager curiosity, it was spiraling down into the heart of a star to observe the integration of helium at first hand.

THE LONG REMEMBERING

POUL ANDERSON

A dark and searching look at one of the unexpected consequences of time travel, from a master science-fiction writer whose knowledge of the prehistoric world is deep and wide-ranging.

Claire took my arm. "Must you go right away?" she asked.

"I'd better," I said. "Don't worry, sweetheart. I'll bring back a nice fat check and tomorrow night we'll celebrate." I stroked her cheek. "You haven't gotten much celebration lately, have you?"

"It doesn't matter," she said. "It's enough just having you around the place." After a moment when we could not have spoken: "Okay. Run along."

She stood in the door and smiled at me all my way down the stairs. During my bus ride, I decided for the thousandth time that I was a lucky fellow in spite of everything.

Rennie's house was big and old, the neighborhood somewhat better than ours. When I rang the bell, he admitted me himself, a tall gray man with tired eyes. "Ah, Mr. Armand," he said gently. "You are punctual. Come in."

He led me down the hall to a cluttered living room where books hid the walls. "Sit down," he invited. "Do you care for a drink?" We were alone, I realized.

"Thank you. A little wine, if you please." I looked out the windows to the undistinguished sunlight. A car went past, the newest and most blatant model. My leather armchair was solid, comfortable; when I moved, its horsehair stuffing rustled. I needed such assurances of everyday reality around me.

Rennie brought in a decanter and poured for us both. The Burgundy was pretty good. He sat down opposite me and crossed interminable legs.

"You can still back out," he said. "I won't think the worse of you." His half-smile faded. "My subjects don't sign those elaborate legal waivers for nothing. And you're married, aren't you?"

I nodded. That was no reason for retreat. Rather, it was my reason for being here. Claire worked, but we had a baby on the way, and as for me, graduate assistants in the chemistry department are not exactly overpaid. Rennie's spectacular experiments in psychophysics had won him a large grant, and he offered good money to volunteers. In a few hours with him, I could earn what would make all the difference to us.

Still . . . "I've never heard of any danger," I said. "You don't send people physically into the past."

"No." He looked beyond me. His words came stiff: "But this is such a new thing . . . full of wild variables. . . . I can't predict how far back you'll go, or what will happen then. Suppose your ancestor has—or had—a bad shock while you're there. What would the effect be on you?"

"Why, uh, has anybody had experiences like that?"

"Yes. No permanent psychological damage resulted, but some did return terrified and needed days to calm down. Others reported no events that were unpleasant *per se*, but nevertheless were deeply, unaccountably depressed for a while afterward. Everyone has, at best, felt disoriented at first. You mustn't expect to accomplish much in the next few days, Mr. Armand."

"I've been warned, sir, and made arrangements." I buried my gaze in the wineglass.

"You should be back to normal within a week. I want you to understand, though, I can promise nothing."

"I do."

"Very well, then." Rennie smiled and leaned back. "Let's get acquainted. I know little about you except that your psycho-profile indicates you'll be an excellent subject. Is your ancestry French?"

I nodded. "From the Dordogne. My parents were over here when I was born because my father worked for the diplomatic corps. I like France, but decided I'd rather be an American."

"Well, you won't necessarily find yourself back there," said Rennie. "The races of Europe are so scrambled. I'm going to try to send you across a longer timespan than the few generations I've managed hitherto." He sipped. "How well do you know the theory of temporal psycho-displacement?"

"Just what I've read in the popular-science magazines and such," I admitted. "Let's see. . . . My world line through the space-time continuum goes back farther than my birth. At the point where I was begotten, it connects to those of my parents, and so on for grandparents, as far as the first living cell on Earth, possibly. The mind, the consciousness, whatever you want to call it, seems to be a function of the world line itself, as well as of the individual body. At least, you've found that under the proper conditions the mind can move back to a different part of the line—or scan back; the theorists are still arguing which, and the theologians are claiming that what's involved is actually the soul."

Rennie chuckled. "Not bad. What's your personal opinion?"

"I don't feel qualified to have any," I said. "What's yours, sir? You insist in public you're suspending judgment till more data come in, but surely the pioneer—"

My voice trailed off in embarrassment. He must have sensed how I admired him, for he said quietly: "Please. I've done nothing more than systematize the work of predecessors, from as long ago as Dunne and Rhine, if not farther. I owe a tremendous debt to Mitchell and his colleagues; in fact, what I've done amounts largely to fusing their discoveries in noetics with some new concepts of physics and cosmology, and using modern laboratory equipment to check out the hypotheses that followed."

"I've wondered—why can't you send me into the future?" I asked.

"I don't know," he replied. "I just can't—so far, anyway. None of the various explanations satisfy me."

He became the parched professor, maybe as a shield: "In spite of the countless news stories you must have seen, Mr. Armand, let me summarize for you the subjective experience you will undergo. Your body will lie unconscious for several hours. Your mind will be in the brain, or scanning the brain, of some ancestor, for the same period of time. But you will not be aware of that, of any separate identity. On arousal—return—you will remember what went on, as if that other person had been you. Nothing more, nothing less."

It was Faustian enough for me. My heart thuttered. "Can we get started soon, please?" I begged.

His laboratory had once been an upstairs bedroom. I loosened my clothes, took off my shoes, stretched on a couch. A pill I took was merely a tranquilizer, the biofeedback exercise merely to establish the desired brain rhythms. Then the laser-drive induction field took over and I fell into night.

I was Argnach-eskaladuan-torkluk, which means He Who Casts the Rope Against the Horse; but my true name I hold secret from warlocks and the wind ghosts, and will not reveal. When my first thin beard sprouted, I got my open name because I lurked near a water hole till a herd of horses came by, then threw a line around one neck, thus holding the beast till I could cut its throat and drag it home. That was on my Journey, which boys make alone. Afterward we are taken off to a certain place in the dark, and the wind ghosts dance in aurochs' hides before us, reindeer-antlered, and the first joint of the left middle finger is cut off and given them to eat. More I may not say. When it is over, we are men and can take wives.

This had happened—I do not know how long ago. The Men

do not count time. But I was still in the pride of my youth. Tonight it was a cold pride, for I went by myself with small hope of coming back.

Snow gusted across my path as I walked down the hillside. Trees, dwarfish and scattered, talked in a huge noisy wind. Afar sounded a lion's roar. Maybe that was the same lion which had eaten Andutannalok-gargut when last the fall season had kindled rain-wet leaves. I shuddered and fingered the Mother charm in my pouch, for I had no wish to meet a beast with Andutannalok's ghost looking out of its eyes.

The storm was waning. I saw low clouds break overhead and stars tremble between sere branches. Still the dry snow hissed by my ankles and crusted in the fur of my clothing. Still there was little save darkness to see; I made my way as hunters do, my whole skin feeling what lay around.

This was in spite of heavy coat, trousers, and boots, whose leathers should be proof against spear thrusts. But the goblins had more strength in their arms than a Man does. Any of them could hurl a stone that would smash my skull like a ripe fruit. And then my body would be left for wolves to devour, and where should my poor gaunt ghost find a home? The wind would harry it through the forests and up over the northern tundra.

I bore weapons: three flint knives at my belt, several spears in a bundle across my shoulder, a throwing-stick in my hand. The foremost spear was tipped with wolf bone to bite the deeper, and Ingmarak the Ghost Man had chanted over it. The rest had keen, fresh-chipped stone points. And my free fingers caressed the great comforting breasts of the Mother. Yet my single companion was the wind.

Trees thickened when I came down into the valley, mostly scrub oak and willow. At last I had woods around me and must part underbrush with arms and shins to pass through. Ahead, the river's brawling began to fill the gloom. Our cave seemed very far behind, unclimbably far in the cliffs.

Nobody there had forbidden me to go after Evavy-unaroa,

my white witch girl. How could they? But all had spoken against it and none would come along. Ingmarak shook his bald head and blinked dim rheumy eyes at me. "This is not well, Argnach," he said. "No good can be found in Goblin Land. Take a new wife."

"I only want Evavy-unaroa," I told him.

The elders mumbled. Children stared frightened from shadowed corners. What thing possessed me? I did not know myself.

I had gotten her only last summer, when my eyes grew suddenly hungry for her and she smiled back on me. No man had had her before, and her father drove an easy bargain. For everyone else was the least bit afraid of her—that dearest, merriest of creatures ever to walk the earth—and still did not ask to borrow her. This suited me, whether or not it lowered my standing a bit. We could afford that, since I was among the best hunters and people liked us both. It was only that other men didn't want to take a needless risk.

Soapstone lamps guttered and flared. Wind flapped the skins hung on poles before the hollow in the cliff where we sat. The fires gave such warmth that folk wore little clothing or none. Near the cave mouth was a good store of meat, gloriously ripening. We should have been cheerful. But when I told them I would go into Goblin Land and fetch Evavy back, fear had walked in and squatted among us.

"They have already eaten her," said Vuotak-nanavo, the one-eyed man who braided his beard and could smell game half a day's walk into the breeze. "Her and the unborn child, they are eaten, and lest their ghosts do not stay in the goblin bellies but come back here, we would do well to lay another hand ax under the hearth she used."

"Perhaps they have not been eaten," I replied. "It is my weird to go."

When I had said this, there was no turning back, and silence dropped from the night. Finally Ingmarak, the Ghost Man, rose. "Tomorrow we will make spells," he said.

We did a great deal on that day and in the twilight. All saw me take a lamp, the twig brushes, and the little pots of paint, deep into the cave. I drew myself overcoming the goblins, and colored my face. What else went on may not be spoken of.

Well, Ingmarak did relate to me at tedious length what I had always known about the goblins. Old stories told how they once held the entire land, till the Men came from the direction of winter sunrise and slowly crowded them out. Now the two kinds seldom glimpsed each other and hardly ever fought. We were afraid to attack them—what unknown powers were theirs?— and ourselves had nothing worth their robbery; they flaked tools somewhat differently from us, but no worse, and seemed to have less need of clothes. The river divided our countries, and few ever crossed it from either side.

But Evavy had gone there to fetch stones from its bed. They were strong stones in that water, for it flowed from the far north, where Father Mammoth walked the tundra and shook his tusks beneath the heights of the Ice. She wanted lucky pebbles to make a necklace for her child when it was born. She went alone because of having secret words to say, carried a spear and a torch against beasts and was not afraid.

When she made no return, I tracked her and in the trampled snow saw what had happened. A goblin party had stolen her. If she still lived, she was on their side of the water.

Now, on my quest, I reached the shore. The stream was broad, a snake of blackness between white banks and icy trees, in spots dully a-shimmer as if scales caught light. This bottom of the valley was sheltered from the wind, which was falling anyhow; but cold breathed from the currents, and I saw ice floes whirl past.

During the day, with proper apologies, I had chopped down a small tree. An ax is not a good weapon, I think, but does make a useful tool. Most branches I had lopped, leaving some which ought to keep me from upsetting and drowning, and one I had made into a rough paddle.

I took off my boots and hung them around my neck. The snow bit my feet like teeth. The clouds were black, sundering mountains above me. Northward the air stood clear and the dead hunters danced in the sky, their many-colored mantles waving and their long spears shaken at the stars. For them, I drew a knife and cut off a lock of hair, stood by the river and said into the dying wind:

"I am Argnach-eskaladuan-torkluk, a man of the Men, who here gives you a piece of his life. For this gift, of course, I ask no return. But know, Star Hunters, I am bound into Goblin Land to fetch back my wife, Evavy-unaroa the white witch girl, and our child that she bears. For any aid I may receive, I offer a fat part of every kill I make for the rest of my days on earth."

The brightnesses flapped huge. The chill gnawed in toward my foot-bones. My voice had come out very small and lonely. So with a grunt, as a man grunts when he spears a boar that may die or may live to slash him apart, I launched my log.

At once the river had me. I sped downstream while I drove my paddle into foam and craziness. The waters roared. I was numbed in the feet, numbed in the head. What happened to me seemed to be happening to a stranger far off while I, the I of my secret name, stood on a high mountain thinking strong thoughts. I thought it was really needless to freeze my feet this way, when by fire and scraping a trunk could be hollowed out for men to sit dry inside and fish or chase marsh fowl.

Then my deadened toes bumped on stones, the log grated in shallows. I sprang off and hauled it ashore after me. For a while I sat rubbing life back into my feet with a fox skin. When that was done, I put on my boots again and started into Goblin Land, marking well the path I took.

We knew where the goblins denned, closer to the river than us on our side. I went at an easy pace, snuffing the almost quiet air for a smoke to guide me. I was somewhat afraid, but not much, because my weird was on me and nothing could change whatever was going to happen. Besides, the whole world had felt not quite real to me since the evening I saw goblin tracks across Evavy's bootprints. It had been as if I were already half a ghost.

I do not understand why I should have lost all wariness toward her, I alone among the Men. They agreed she was tall and well-shaped, brave of heart, skilled of hand, and free with her laughter. But she had blue eyes and yellow hair like a goblin. Folk did say, to be sure, that of old, matings had taken place between the two breeds, so that now and again the light-hued strain appeared in us; but no one alive could remember another such child. Thus a Power clearly dwelt in Evavy-unaroa, and while she gave no reason to suppose it was harmful, still, nobody was quite sure what might come of coupling with her, and shied off from taking the chance.

I, Argnach, had not. My spirit saw that her Power was the Mother's and could only be good. Now I knew that it was, as well, the same which makes a bull elk stand and die for his mates.

The racket of a herd, alarmed by something and crashing off through young trees, put that thought in me. A dim wintry light had begun to steal between the boughs. I spied signs of plentiful game, more than we had on our side of the river. Much more!

And we were breeding more mouths than men who hunted, boys who fished, women and girls who gathered could readily feed.

I came out on an open slope, grassy in summer, which climbed northward to bulk wan across the last stars. A low breeze brought me smoke. My flesh prickled. I was near the goblin haunt.

If they were indeed such warlocks as the stories told of, they would soon smite me. I would fall dead, or turn into a worm and be crushed underfoot, or run screaming and foaming into the woods as some have done who were never seen again.

But Evavy was yonder, if she lived.

Therefore I made myself into smoke, drifting amidst shadows, curling behind boulders, winding from bush to thicket to tussock, throwing-stick in my left hand and foremost spear in my right. The eastern sky had blanched when I saw the goblin cave.

It was bigger and wider-mouthed than ours. They did not make a shelter outside and mostly use that, like us. Instead, they stayed inside and kept a fire always at the entrance. Ingmarak had told me that in his childhood the Men had done the same, but this was no longer needful; the beasts had learned not to approach us. Hereabouts were more beasts than in our country, and they must be bolder. I had supposed the abundance came from goblin spells, raising game out of dawn mists. But as I stood and peered through the branches of a low-sweeping juniper, a very great thought came to me.

"If they have the Power," I whispered to myself, "then they should not be afraid of lion or bear. They should not need a fire in front of their home. But they do. Then perhaps, O Star Hunters, this is because they do not have the Power. Perhaps they are not even such good hunters as the Men, and that is the reason there are many animals in their land."

I shuddered with the thought, strength lifted in me, I had no more fear at all.

Most softly, then, I stole over the last stretch to the goblin lair.

An old one was tending the fire. This was the first time I had seen any at close range. The sight was less dreadful than I had awaited. He was much shorter than I, thickly shaped, but would have been as erect had age not stooped and gnarled him. His hair, once tawny, hung grizzled and unkempt past his shoulders, which were still broad, the arms on them still brawny. His head was the strangest part, long, flattened on top, low of brow, eyes nearly lost under great ridges, no chin behind the thin beard.

He stamped his feet, beat hands together, puffed frost out of a craglike nose. Well must he be cold, for his dress was no more than a few hides clumsily lashed to each other and to him, while his feet were bare. He stayed alert, though. When I broke from cover and sped across the last few man-lengths, he yelled and snatched for a club.

My spear butt seemed of itself to find the angle of the throwing-stick. The cast whirred. The wolf bone struck. The goblin lurched, clutched at the shaft in his belly, fell onto the snow where his blood shouted louder than his pain. I sprang past him to the cave mouth, drew a second spear from my harness, and roared for Evavy.

A goblin came out with a spear of his own. Its point was merely fire-hardened. Outreaching him, I stabbed mine in. A third male lifted a hand ax; they don't make the hafted kind. Before I could unlimber a fresh weapon, but also before he could smite, I seized a brand from the fire and thrust. The flame drew a wail from him. He fell backward to escape more.

It boiled with naked bodies in there. I dimly glimpsed the squat, ugly women scramble rearward, to guard their cubs and clash teeth at me. The goblin men bumbled in half-darkness, crying out, and the knowledge thrilled in me that they were afraid.

"Evavy!" I called. "Evavy, Argnach is come for you!"

Through one lost heartbeat, I knew fear again, that her ghost would answer from a goblin mouth. Then she had pushed her way to the front. I looked into eyes like summer's heaven, and tears stung my own.

"This way!" I loosed a spear blind into the murk. A goblin yelped. "Run!" I said needlessly.

Our flight must have heartened them. They pounded after us, howling and grunting. Evavy's feet paced mine, her hair streamed near my face. They had not taken her clothes, but even through the heavy furs I could see the grace of her, even then I savored it.

Down the slope we dashed, into the forest. Soon a deer trail helped us draw farther ahead of pursuit. They could not run as fast as Men. Once, when we crossed a glade, a stone whooped past me with more speed than I could have given it. But no spears came close.

Breath was harsh and hot in our throats by the time we reached the riverside where my log waited. "Get that launched!" I ordered. We could not hope to swim this icy torrent. While she strained at the weight, I leaned my remaining spears against a bole—none too early.

The goblins burst out of crackly, glittery brush. I wounded two of them. A third got in arm's length, caught the shaft I had, and wrenched it from me. I drew a knife and slashed him. Someone else stabbed at me, but my leather coat turned the wooden point. Evavy took a spear and jabbed back, hurting the naked creature. The goblins roiled in withdrawal from us. Our log was almost afloat. We waded, gave a last push, straddled it, and were in the river's arms.

I looked behind. The goblins hopped about, yelled, shook fists. Whatever fallen tree they had come raiding on was nowhere near, and the current had borne us out of casting range—swiftly bore us around a bend and out of sight. I laughed aloud and dug my paddle deep.

Evavy wept. "But you are free!" I said.

"That is why I weep," she answered. The Earth Powers are strong and strange in womankind.

"Did they hurt you?" I asked.

"No," she said. "One of them . . . I had seen before, watching me from his side. He and a few caught me by surprise and brought me across to their cave. They would not let me go. But they did no harm, did not even mount me; they gave me their best food and crooned gentle, unknown words. Yet I could not go back to you—" She wept afresh.

I thought that her fair coloring must indeed have made her a lovely sight to the goblins, as she was to me, while her height and features lent wonder, yes, mystery. They must have reckoned it well worth the risk to have her for—what? Their Mother?

I stopped my toil to stroke her hair. "There has been a weird in this," I said. "We were afraid of the goblins because they look so strange—we thought they must command a Power."

The river hallooed in the first long light of the sun. My paddle wrestled the water again. "But that is not true," I said. "They are poor and awkward folk, slow on their feet and slow in their souls. Our fathers who hunt in the sky on winter nights drove the goblins off—not with spears or axes, I believe, but because they could think more widely and run more swiftly. Thus they could kill more game and raise more children. The goblins must leave or starve.

"Now we are outgrowing our grounds. When summer comes, I will gather the Men and cross the river. We will take those lands too for our own."

We struck the shallows on the home side and waded ashore. Evavy clung to me, her teeth clapping in her head. I wanted to make haste, back to the fires before the cave and the victory song I would sing for the Men. But a sound drew my gaze back across the water.

The goblins had reappeared there. They stood clustered, staring and staring. One of them reached out his arms. He was a goodly ways from me, but I have sharp eyes and saw his tears.

Because he also cares for Evavy, I will try to spare his life when we cross the river.

I came awake. A fluorescent lamp shone pale, for night lay beyond the drawn curtains.

Rennie guided me back to the living room and offered his wine. I had spoken no word.

"Well?" he said at last. "Where . . . when did you go?"

"A hell of a long way," I answered from the dream which still had me.

"Yes?" His look smoldered.

"I don't know the date. Let the archaeologists figure it out." In a few sentences I told him what had happened.

"My God," he whispered. "The Old Stone Age. Twenty thousand years ago, maybe, when half the northern hemisphere lay under the glacier." He reached out to grip my arm.

"You have seen the first true human beings, the Crô-Magnon people, and the last Neanderthal ape-men."

"No, wrong," I muttered. "The difference wasn't that big between them. I feel sorry for the Neanderthals. They tried hard. . . . Look, I'm dazed. Can I go home and sleep it off?"

"Certainly. Typical reaction. You'll come back tomorrow, won't you? I want to record a full statement from you. Everything you can remember—everything! Good Lord, I never imagined you'd go so far."

He escorted me to the door. "Can you make your way all right?" he asked.

"Yes. I'm okay. Okay enough, anyhow." We shook hands.

"Good night." His tall form stood black in the yellow-lit doorway.

The bus I wanted stopped at the corner within minutes. When I had boarded, it rumbled and whined so that for a moment fear tensed my guts. What monster was this, what alien stenches? Then I remembered I'd inhabited the skin of another man, who was twenty thousand years in his grave.

That did not at once make the world come real. I walked through a winter wood where elk bugled, while ghosts crowded around me and twittered in my ear.

Climbing the stairs in my apartment building restored a measure of solidity. I swung aside an unlocked door and entered our general-purpose room. Claire put down a cigarette, rose from her chair, and came to me. "How are you, darling?" Her tone trembled. "How'd everything go?"

"Not too bad. Fantastic, in fact." I braced myself. "Except I'm bushed. Before I tell you, how about some coffee?"

"Of course, of course. But where did you *go*, darling?" She dragged me by the hand toward the kitchenette.

I considered her, clean, kindly, a trifle plump, rouged, creamed, girdled, with glasses and carefully waved hair and tobacco stale upon her breath. A face rose before me that was brown from sun and wind, weather-bleached yellow mane, eyes like summer's heaven. I remembered freckles dusted across a nose lifted sooty from the cookfire, and low laughter and work-hardened small hands reaching for me. And I knew what my punishment was for what I had done, and knew it would never end.

TRY AND CHANGE THE PAST

FRITZ LEIBER

A classic theme of science fiction is the one about the time-traveler whose journey into the past inadvertently causes immense changes in history—as, for example, William Tenn's lovely story "Brooklyn Project," or Ray Bradbury's "A Sound of Thunder." But there's no theme so sacred that it can't be subjected to a closer look—and when the taker of that second look is a writer of the stature of Fritz Leiber, accepted concepts are apt to undergo some severe reassessments.

No, I wouldn't advise anyone to try to change the past, at least not his *personal* past, although changing the *general* past is my business, my fighting business. You see, I'm a Snake in the Change War. Don't back off—human beings, even Resurrected ones engaged in time-fighting, aren't built for outward wriggling and their poison is mostly psychological. "Snake" is slang for the soldiers on our side, like Hun or Reb or Ghibelline. In the Change War we're trying to alter the past—and it's tricky, brutal work, believe me—at points all over the cosmos, anywhere and anywhen, so that history will be warped to make our side defeat the Spiders. But that's a much bigger story, the biggest, in fact, and I'll leave it occupying several planets of

93

microfilm and two asteroids of coded molecules in the files of the High Command.

Change one event in the past and you get a brand new future? Erase the conquests of Alexander by nudging a Neolithic pebble? Extirpate America by pulling up a shoot of Sumerian grain? Brother, that isn't the way it works at all! The space-time continuum's built of stubborn stuff, and change is anything but a chain reaction. Change the past and you start a wave of changes moving futurewards, but it damps out mighty fast. Haven't you ever heard of temporal reluctance, or of the Law of the Conservation of Reality?

Here's a little story that will illustrate my point: This guy was fresh recruited, the Resurrection sweat still wet in his armpits, when he got the idea he'd use the time-traveling power to go back and make a couple of little changes in his past so that his life would take a happier course and maybe, he thought, he wouldn't have to die and get mixed up with Snakes and Spiders at all. It was as if a new-enlisted feuding hill-billy soldier should light out with the high-power rifle they issued him to go back to his mountains and pick off his pet enemies.

Normally it couldn't ever have happened. Normally, to avoid just this sort of thing, he'd have been shipped straight off to some place a few thousand or million years distant from his point of enlistment and maybe a few light-years, too. But there was a local crisis in the Change War and a lot of routine operations got held up and one new recruit was simply forgotten.

Normally, too, he'd never have been left alone a moment in the Dispatching Room, never even have glimpsed the place except to be rushed through it on arrival and reshipment. But, as I say, there happened to be a crisis, the Snakes were shorthanded, and several soldiers were careless. Afterwards two N.C.'s were busted because of what happened and a First Looey not only lost his commission but was transferred outside the galaxy and the era. But during the crisis this recruit I'm telling you about had opportunity and more to fool around with forbidden things and try out his schemes.

He also had all the details on the last part of his life back on the real world, on his death and its consequences, to mull over and be tempted to change. This wasn't anybody's carelessness. The Snakes give every candidate that information as part of the recruiting pitch. They spot a death coming and the Resurrection Men go back and recruit the person from a point a few minutes or at most a few hours earlier. They explain in uncomfortable detail what's going to happen and wouldn't he rather take the oath and put on scales? I never heard of anybody turning down that offer. Then they lift him from his lifeline in the form of a Doubleganger and from then on, brother, he's a Snake.

So this guy had a clearer picture of his death than of the day he bought his first car, and a masterpiece of morbid irony it was. He was living in a classy penthouse that had belonged to a crazy uncle of his—it even had a midget astronomical observatory, unused for years—but he was stony broke, up to the top hair in debt, and due to be dispossessed next day. He'd never had a real job, always lived off his rich relatives and his wife's, but now he was getting a little too mature for his stern dedication to a life of sponging to be cute. His charming personality, which had been his only asset, was deader from overuse and abuse than he himself would be in a few hours. His crazy uncle would not have anything to do with him any more. His wife was responsible for a lot of the wear and tear on his social-butterfly wings; she had hated him for years, had screamed at him morning to night the way you can only get away with in a penthouse, and was going batty herself. He'd been playing around with another woman, who'd just given him the gate, though he knew his wife would never believe that and would only add a scornful note to her screaming if she did.

It was a lousy evening, smack in the middle of an August heat wave. The Giants were playing a night game with Brooklyn. Two long-run musicals had closed. Wheat had hit a new high. There was a brush fire in California and a war scare in Iran. And tonight a meteor shower was due, according to an astronomical bulletin that had arrived in the morning mail addressed to his uncle—he generally dumped such stuff in the fireplace unopened, but today he had looked at it because he had nothing else to do, either more useful or more interesting.

The phone rang. It was a lawyer. His crazy uncle was dead and in the will there wasn't a word about an Asteroid Search Foundation. Every penny of the fortune went to the no-good nephew.

This same character finally hung up the phone, fighting off a tendency for his heart to spring giddily out of his chest and through the ceiling. Just then his wife came screeching out of the bedroom. She'd received a cute, commiserating, tell-all note from the other woman; she had a gun and announced that she was going to finish him off.

The sweltering atmosphere provided a good background for sardonic catastrophe. The French doors to the roof were open behind him but the air that drifted through was muggy as death. Unnoticed, a couple of meteors streaked faintly across the night sky.

Figuring it would sure dissuade her, he told her about the inheritance. She screamed that he'd just use the money to buy more other women—not an unreasonable prediction—and pulled the trigger.

The danger was minimal. She was at the other end of a big living room, her hand wasn't just shaking, she was waving the nickel-plate revolver as if it were a fan.

The bullet took him right between the eyes. He flopped down, deader than his hopes were before he got the phone call. He saw it happen because as a clincher the Resurrection Men brought him forward as a Doubleganger to witness it invisibly—also standard Snake procedure and not productive of time-complications, incidentally, since Doublegangers don't imprint on reality unless they want to.

They stuck around a bit. His wife looked at the body for a couple of seconds, went to her bedroom, blonded her graying hair by dousing it with two bottles of undiluted peroxide, put on a tarnished gold-lamé evening gown and a bucket of makeup, went back to the living room, sat down at the piano, played "Country Gardens" and then shot herself, too.

So that was the little skit, the little double blackout he had to mull over outside the empty and unguarded Dispatching Room, quite forgotten by its twice-depleted skeleton crew while every available Snake in the sector was helping deal with the local crisis, which centered around the planet Alpha Centauri Four, two million years minus.

Naturally it didn't take him long to figure out that if he went back and gimmicked things so that the first blackout didn't occur, but the second still did, he would be sitting pretty back in the real world and able to devote his inheritance to fulfilling his wife's prediction and other pastimes. He didn't know much about Doublegangers yet and had it figured out that if he didn't die in the real world, he'd have no trouble resuming his existence there—maybe it'd even happen automatically.

So this Snake—name kind of fits him, doesn't it?—crossed his fingers and slipped into the Dispatching Room. Dispatching is so simple a child could learn it in five minutes from studying the board. He went back to a point a couple of hours before the tragedy, carefully avoiding the spot where the Resurrection Men had lifted him from his lifeline. He found the revolver in a dresser drawer, unloaded it, checked to make sure there weren't any more cartridges around, and then went ahead a couple of hours, arriving just in time to see himself get the slug between the eyes same as before.

As soon as he got over his disappointment, he realized he'd learned something about Doublegangers he should have known all along, if his mind had been clicking. The bullets he'd lifted were Doublegangers, too; they had disappeared from the real world only at the point in space-time where he'd lifted them, and they had continued to exist, as real as ever, in the earlier and later sections of their lifelines—with the result that the gun was loaded again by the time his wife had grabbed it up.

So this time he set the board so he'd arrive just a few minutes before the tragedy. He lifted the gun, bullets and all, and waited around to make sure it stayed lifted. He figured—rightly—that if he left this space-time sector, the gun would reappear in the dresser drawer, and he didn't want his wife getting hold of any gun, even one with a broken lifeline. Afterwards—after his own death was averted, that is—he figured he'd put the gun back in his wife's hands.

Two things reassured him a lot, although he'd been expecting the one and hoping for the other: his wife didn't notice his presence as a Doubleganger, and when she went to grab the gun she acted as if it weren't gone and held her right hand just as if there were a gun in it. If he'd studied philosophy, he'd have realized he was witnessing a proof of Liebniz's theory of Pre-established harmony: that neither atoms nor human beings really affect each other, they just look as if they did.

But anyway he had no time for theories. Still holding the gun, he drifted out into the living room to get a box seat right next to Himself for the big act. Himself didn't notice him any more than his wife had.

His wife came out and spoke her piece same as ever, Himself cringed as if she still had the gun and started to babble about the inheritance, his wife sneered and made as if she were shooting Himself.

Sure enough, there was no shot this time, *and* no mysteriously appearing bullet hole—which was something he'd been afraid of. Himself just stood there dully while his wife made as if she were looking down at a dead body and went back to her bedroom.

He was pretty pleased: this time he actually *had* changed the past. Then Himself slowly glanced around at him, still with that dull look, and slowly came toward him. He was more pleased than ever because he figured now they'd melt together into one man and one lifeline again, and he'd be able to hurry out somewhere and establish an alibi, just to be on the safe side, while his wife suicided.

But it didn't happen quite that way. Himself's look changed from dull to desperate, he came up close . . . and suddenly grabbed the gun and quick as a wink put a thumb to the trigger and shot himself between the eyes. And flopped, same as ever.

Right there he was starting to learn a little—and it was an unpleasant, shivery sort of learning—about the Law of the Conservation of Reality. The four-dimensional space-time universe doesn't *like* to be changed, any more than it likes to lose or gain energy or matter. If it *has* to be changed, it'll adjust itself just enough to accept that change and no more. The Conservation of Reality is a sort of Law of Least Action, too. It doesn't matter how improbable the events involved in the adjustment are, just as long as they're possible at all and can be used to patch the established pattern. His death, at this point, was part of the established pattern. If he lived on instead of dying, billions of other compensatory changes would have to be made, covering many years, perhaps centuries, before the old pattern could be re-established, the snarled lifelines woven back into it—and the universe finally go on the same as if his wife had shot him on schedule.

This way the pattern was hardly affected at all. There were powder burns on his forehead that weren't there before, but there weren't any witnesses to the shooting in the first place, so the presence or absence of powder burns didn't matter. The gun was lying on the floor instead of being in his wife's hands, but he had the feeling that when the time came for her to die, she'd wake enough from the Pre-established Harmony trance to find it, just as Himself did.

So he'd learned a little about the Conservation of Reality. He also had learned a little about his own character, especially from Himself's last look and act. He'd got a hint that he had been trying to destroy himself for years by the way he'd lived, so that inherited fortune or accidental success couldn't save him, and if his wife hadn't shot him he'd have done it himself in any case. He'd got a hint that Himself hadn't merely been acting as an agent for a self-correcting universe when he grabbed the gun, he'd been acting on his own account, too—the universe, you know, operates by getting people to co-operate.

But, although these ideas occurred to him, he didn't dwell on them, for he figured he'd had a partial success the second time, and the third time if he kept the gun away from Himself, if he dominated Himself, as it were, the melting-together would take place and everything else go forward as planned.

He had the dim realization that the universe, like a huge sleepy animal, knew what he was trying to do and was trying to thwart him. This feeling of opposition made him determined to outmaneuver the universe—not the first guy to yield to such a temptation, of course.

And up to a point his tactics worked. The third time he gimmicked the past, everything started to happen just as it did the second time. Himself dragged miserably over to him, looking for the gun, but he had it tucked away and was prepared to hold on to it. Encouragingly, Himself didn't grapple, the look of desperation changed to one of utter hopelessness, and Himself turned away from him and very slowly walked to the French doors and stood looking out into the sweating night. He figured Himself was just getting used to the idea of not dying. There wasn't a breath of air. A couple of meteors streaked across the sky. Then, mixed with the upseeping night sounds of the city, there was a low whirring whistle.

Himself shook a bit, as if he'd had a sudden chill. Then Himself turned around and slumped to the floor in one movement. Between his eyes was a black hole.

Then and there this Snake I'm telling you about decided

never again to try and change the past, at least not his personal past. He'd had it, and he'd also acquired a healthy respect for a High Command able to change the past, albeit with difficulty. He scooted back to the Dispatching Room, where a sleepy and surprised Snake gave him a terrific chewing-out and confined him to quarters. The chewing-out didn't bother him too much—he'd acquired a certain fatalism about things. A person's got to learn to accept reality as it is, you know—just as you'd best not be surprised at the way I disappear in a moment or two—I'm a Snake too, remember.

If a statistician is looking for an example of a highly improbable event, he can hardly pick a more vivid one than the chance of a man being hit by a meteorite. And, if he adds the condition that the meteorite hit him between the eyes so as to counterfeit the wound made by a 32-caliber bullet, the improbability becomes astronomical cubed. So how's a person going to outmaneuver a universe that finds it easier to drill a man through the head that way rather than postpone the date of his death?

DIVINE MADNESS
ROGER ZELAZNY

Wherein the eloquent author of Lord of Light, This Immortal, *"A Rose for Ecclesiastes," and many another celebrated work of science fiction demonstrates that there's more than one direction in which trips in time can be taken.*

"... I IS THIS *?hearers wounded-wonder like stand them makes and stars wandering the conjures sorrow of phrase* Whose ..."

He blew smoke through the cigarette and it grew longer.

He glanced at the clock and realized that its hands were moving backwards.

Then came the thing like despair, for he knew there was not a thing he could do about it. He was trapped, moving in reverse through the sequence of actions past. Somehow, he had missed the warning.

Usually, there was a prism-effect, a flash of pink static, a drowsiness, then a moment of heightened perception . . .

He turned the pages, from left to right, his eyes retracing their path back along the lines.

"?emphasis an such bears grief whose he is What"

Helpless, there behind his eyes, he watched his body perform.

The cigarette had reached its full length. He clicked on the lighter, which sucked away its glowing point, and then he shook the cigarette back into the pack.

He yawned in reverse: first an exhalation, then an inhalation.

It wasn't real—the doctor had told him. It was grief and epilepsy, meeting to form an unusual syndrome.

He'd already had the seizure. The Dilantin wasn't helping. This was a post-traumatic locomotor hallucination, elicited by anxiety, precipitated by the attack.

But he did not believe it, could not believe it—not after twenty minutes had gone by, in the other direction—not after he had placed the book upon the reading stand, stood, walked backward across the room to his closet, hung up his robe, redressed himself in the same shirt and slacks he had worn all day, backed over to the bar and regurgitated a Martini, sip by cooling sip, until the glass was filled to the brim and not a drop spilled.

There was an impending taste of olive, and then everything was changed again.

The second-hand was sweeping around his wristwatch in the proper direction.

The time was 10:07 P.M.

He felt free to move as he wished.

He redrank his Martini.

Now, if he would be true to the pattern, he would change into his robe and try to read. Instead, he mixed another drink.

Now the sequence would not occur.

Now the things would not happen as he thought they had happened, and un-happened.

Now everything was different.

All of which went to prove it had been a hallucination.

Even the notion that it had taken twenty-six minutes each way was an attempted rationalization.

Nothing had happened.

. . . Shouldn't be drinking, he decided. It might bring on a seizure.
He laughed.
Crazy, though, the whole thing . . .
Remembering, he drank.

In the morning he skipped breakfast, as usual, noted that it would soon stop being morning, took two aspirins, a lukewarm shower, a cup of coffee, and a walk.

The park, the fountain, the children with their boats, the grass, the pond, he hated them; and the morning, and the sunlight, and the blue moats around the towering clouds.

Hating, he sat there. And remembering.

If he was on the verge of a crackup, he decided, then the thing he wanted most was to plunge ahead into it, not to totter halfway out, halfway in.

He remembered why.

But it was clear, so clear, the morning, and everything crisp and distinct and burning with the green fires of spring, there in the sign of the Ram, April.

He watched the winds pile up the remains of winter against the far gray fence, and he saw them push the boats across the pond, to come to rest in shallow mud the children tracked.

The fountain jetted its cold umbrella above the green-tinged copper dolphins. The sun ignited it whenever he moved his head. The wind rumpled it.

Clustered on the concrete, birds pecked at part of a candy bar stuck to a red wrapper.

Kites swayed on their tails, nosed downward, rose again, as youngsters tugged at invisible strings. Telephone lines were tangled with wooden frames and torn paper, like broken G clefs and smeared glissandos.

He hated the telephone lines, the kites, the children, the birds.

Most of all, though, he hated himself.

How does a man undo that which has been done? He doesn't. There is no way under the sun. He may suffer, remember, repeat, curse, or forget. Nothing else. The past, in this sense, is inevitable.

A woman walked past. He did not look up in time to see her face, but the dusky blond fall of her hair to her collar and the swell of her sure, sheer-netted legs below the black hem of her coat and above the matching click of her heels heigh-ho stopped his breath behind his stomach and snared his eyes in the wizard-welt of her walking and her posture and some more, like a rhyme to the last of his thoughts.

He half-rose from the bench when the pink static struck his eyeballs, and the fountain became a volcano spouting rainbows.

The world was frozen and served up to him under glass.

. . . The woman passed back before him and he looked down too soon to see her face.

The hell was beginning once more, he realized, as the backward-flying birds passed before.

He gave himself to it. Let it keep him until he broke, until he was all used up and there was nothing left.

He waited, there on the bench, watching the slithy toves be brillig, as the fountain sucked its waters back within itself, drawing them up in a great arc above the unmoving dolphins, and the boats raced backward across the pond, and the fence divested itself of stray scraps of paper, as the birds replaced the candy bar within the red wrapper, bit by crunchy bit.

His thoughts only were inviolate, his body belonged to the retreating tide.

Eventually, he rose and strolled backwards out of the park.

On the street a boy backed past him, unwhistling snatches of a popular song.

He backed up the stairs to his apartment, his hangover growing worse again, undrank his coffee, unshowered, unswallowed his aspirins, and got into bed, feeling awful.

Let this be it, he decided.

A faintly remembered nightmare ran in reverse through his mind, giving it an undeserved happy ending.

It was dark when he awakened.

He was very drunk.

He backed over to the bar and began spitting out his drinks, one by one into the same glass he had used the night before, and pouring them from the glass back into the bottles again. Separating the gin and vermouth was no trick at all. The proper liquids leaped into the air as he held the uncorked bottles above the bar.

And he grew less and less drunk as this went on.

Then he stood before an early Martini and it was 10:07 P.M. There, within the hallucination, he wondered about another hallucination. Would time loop-the-loop, forward and then backward again, through his previous seizure?

No.

It was as though it had not happened, had never been.

He continued on back through the evening, undoing things.

He raised the telephone, said "good-bye," untold Murray that he would not be coming to work again tomorrow, listened a moment, recradled the phone and looked at it as it rang.

The sun came up in the west and people were backing their cars to work.

He read the weather report and the headlines, folded the evening paper and placed it out in the hall.

It was the longest seizure he had ever had, but he did not really care. He settled himself down within it and watched as the day unwound itself back to morning.

His hangover returned as the day grew smaller, and it was terrible when he got into bed again.

When he awakened the previous evening, the drunkenness was high upon him. Two of the bottles he refilled, recorked, resealed. He knew he would take them to the liquor store soon and get his money back.

As he sat there that day, his mouth uncursing and undrinking and his eyes unreading, he knew that new cars were being shipped back to Detroit and disassembled, that corpses were awakening into their death-throes, and that priests the world over were saying black mass, unknowing.

He wanted to chuckle, but he could not tell his mouth to do it.

He unsmoked two and a half packs of cigarettes.

Then came another hangover and he went to bed. Later, the sun set in the east.

Time's winged chariot fled before him as he opened the door and said "good-bye" to his comforters and they came in and sat down and told him not to grieve overmuch.

And he wept without tears as he realized what was to come.

Despite his madness, he hurt.

. . . Hurt, as the days rolled backward.

. . . Backward, inexorably.

. . . Inexorably, until he knew the time was near at hand.

He gnashed the teeth of his mind.

Great was his grief and his hate and his love.

He was wearing his black suit and undrinking drink after drink, while somewhere the men were scraping the clay back onto the shovels which would be used to undig the grave.

He backed his car to the funeral parlor, parked it, and climbed into the limousine.

They backed all the way to the graveyard.

He stood among his friends and listened to the preacher.

".dust to dust; ashes to Ashes," the man said, which is pretty much the same whichever way you say it.

The casket was taken back to the hearse and returned to the funeral parlor.

He sat through the service and went home and unshaved and unbrushed his teeth and went to bed.

He awakened and dressed again in black and returned to the parlor.

The flowers were all back in place.

Solemn-faced friends unsigned the Sympathy Book and unshook his hand. Then they went inside to sit awhile and stare at the closed casket. Then they left, until he was alone with the funeral director.

Then he was alone with himself.

The tears ran up his cheeks.

His suit and shirt were crisp and unwrinkled again.

He backed home, undressed, uncombed his hair. The day collapsed around him into morning, and he returned to bed to unsleep another night.

The previous evening, when he awakened, he realized where he was headed.

Twice, he exerted all of his willpower in an attempt to interrupt the sequence of events. He failed.

He wanted to die. If he had killed himself that day, he would not be headed back toward it now.

There were tears within his mind as he realized the past which lay less than twenty-four hours before him.

The past stalked him that day as he unnegotiated the purchase of the casket, the vault, the accessories.

Then he headed home into the biggest hangover of all and slept until he was awakened to undrink drink after drink and then return to the morgue and come back in time to hang up the telephone on that call, that call which had come to break . . .

. . . The silence of his anger with its ringing.

She was dead.

She was lying somewhere in the fragments of her car on Interstate 90 now.

DIVINE MADNESS

As he paced, unsmoking, he knew she was lying there bleeding.

. . . Then dying, after that crash at eighty miles an hour.

. . . Then alive?

Then re-formed, along with the car, and alive again, arisen? Even now backing home at a terrible speed, to re-slam the door on their final argument? To unscream at him and to be unscreamed at?

He cried out within his mind. He wrung the hands of his spirit.

It couldn't stop at this point. No. Not now.

All his grief and his love and his self-hate had brought him back this far, this near to the moment. . . .

It *couldn't* end now.

After a time, he moved to the living room, his legs pacing, his lips cursing, himsef waiting.

The door slammed open.

She stared in at him, her mascara smeared, tears upon her cheeks.

"!hell to go Then," he said.

"!going I'm," she said.

She stepped back inside, closed the door.

She hung her coat hurriedly in the hall closet.

".it about feel you way the that's If," he said, shrugging.

"!yourself but anybody about care don't You," she said.

"!child a like behaving You're," he said.

"!sorry you're say least at could You"

Her eyes flashed like emeralds through the pink static, and she was lovely and alive again. In his mind he was dancing.

The change came.

"You could at least say you're sorry!"

"I am," he said, taking her hand in a grip that she could not break. "How much, you'll never know."

"Come here." And she did.

MUGWUMP 4
ROBERT SILVERBERG

The trouble with science fiction is that it has a hard time keeping up with reality. When I wrote this story, all the way back in the misty Pleistocene days of 1959, telephone numbers in the United States consisted of two-letter prefixes plus five digits–MU 4-1111, PR 2-0545, CI 5-5500– and to make it easier on the memory, the phone company gave us a handy word for each prefix, such as MUrray Hill, PResident, CIrcle. How was I to know that within a few years all our beloved prefixes would be abolished and seven-digit telephone numbers would spread like measles across the land? And today only readers above a certain age remember them at all. So MUrray Hill 4 is now a prosaic 684, and MUgwump 4 the same. But that has no real effect on the events of this story. If anything, Al Miller's time-travel predicament is all the more likely to happen today, in our dazzling world of computerized communications, than in the quaint old days when telephone numbers still had a few letters in them.

Al Miller was only trying to phone the Friendly Finance Corporation to ask about an extension on his loan. It was a Murray Hill number, and he had dialed as far as MU-4 when the receiver clicked queerly and a voice said, "Come in, Operator Nine. Operator Nine, do you read me?"

Al frowned. "I didn't want the operator. There must be something wrong with my phone if—"

"Just a minute. Who *are* you?"

"I ought to ask *you* that," Al said. "What are you doing on the other end of my phone, anyway? I hadn't even finished dialing. I got as far as MU-4 and —"

"Well? You dialed MUgwump 4 and you got us. What more do you want?" A suspicious pause. "Say, you aren't Operator Nine!"

"No, I'm *not* Operator Nine, and I'm trying to dial a Murray Hill number, and how about getting off the line?"

"Hold it, friend. Are you a Normal?"

Al blinked. "Yeah—yeah, I like to think so."

"So how'd you know the Number?"

"Dammit, I *didn't* know the number! I was trying to call someone, and all of a sudden the phone cut out and I got you, whoever the blazes *you* are."

"I'm the communications warden at MUgwump 4," the other said crisply. "And you're a suspicious individual. We'll have to investigate you."

The telephone emitted a sudden burping sound. Al felt as if his feet had grown roots. He could not move at all. It was awkward to be standing there at his own telephone in the privacy of his own room, as unbending as the Apollo Belvedere. Time still moved, he saw. The hand on the big clock above the phone had just shifted from 3:30 to 3:31.

Sweat rivered down his back as he struggled to put down the phone. He fought to lift his left foot. He strained to twitch his right eyelid. No go on all counts; he was frozen, all but his chest muscles—thank goodness for that. He still could breathe.

A few minutes later matters became even more awkward when his front door, which had been locked, opened abruptly. Three strangers entered. They looked oddly alike: a trio of

Tweedledums, no more than five feet high, each wide through the waist, jowly of face and balding of head, each wearing an inadequate single-breasted blue-serge suit.

Al discovered he could roll his eyes. He rolled them. He wanted to apologize because his unexpected paralysis kept him from acting the proper part of a host, but his tongue would not obey. And on second thought, it occurred that the little bald men might be connected in some way with that paralysis.

The reddest-faced of the three little men made an intricate gesture and the stasis ended. Al nearly folded up as the tension that gripped him broke. He said, "Just who the deuce—"

"*We* will ask the questions. You are Al Miller?"

Al nodded.

"And obviously you are a Normal. So there has been a grave error. Mordecai, examine the telephone."

The second little man picked up the phone and calmly disemboweled it with three involved motions of his stubby hands. He frowned over the telephone's innards for a moment; then, humming tunelessly, he produced a wire-clipper and severed the telephone cord.

"Hold on here," Al burst out. "You can't just rip out my phone like that! You aren't from the phone company!"

"Quiet," said the spokesman nastily. "Well, Mordecai?"

The second little man said, "Probability one to a million. The cranch interval overlapped and his telephone matrix slipped. His call was piped into our wire by error, Waldemar."

"So he isn't a spy?" Waldemar asked.

"Doubtful. As you see, he's of rudimentary intelligence. His dialing our number was a statistical fluke."

"But now he knows about Us," said the third little man in a surprisingly deep voice. "I vote for demolecularization."

The other two whirled on their companion. "Always bloodthirsty, eh, Giovanni?" said Mordecai. "You'd violate the Code at the snap of a meson."

"There won't be any demolecularization while *I'm* in charge," added Waldemar.

"What do we do with him, then?" Giovanni demanded.

Mordecai said, "Freeze him and take him down to Headquarters. He's *their* problem."

"I think this has gone about as far as it's going to go," Al exploded at last. "However you three creeps got in here, you'd better get yourselves right out again, or—"

"Enough," Waldemar said. He stamped his foot. Al felt his jaws stiffen. He realized bewilderedly that he was frozen again. And frozen, this time, with his mouth gaping foolishly open.

The trip took about five minutes, and so far as Al was concerned, it was one long blur. At the end of the journey the blur lifted for an instant, just enough to give Al one good glimpse of his surroundings—a residential street in what might have been Brooklyn or Queens (or Cincinnati or Detroit, he thought morbidly) —before he was hustled into the basement of a two-family house. He found himself in a windowless, brightly lit chamber cluttered with complex-looking machinery and with a dozen or so alarmingly identical little bald-headed men.

The chubbiest of the bunch glared sourly at him and asked, "Are you a spy?"

"I'm just an innocent bystander. I picked up my phone and started to dial, and all of a sudden some guy asked me if I was Operator Nine. Honest, that's all."

"Overlapping of the cranch interval," muttered Mordecai. "Slipped matrix."

"Umm. Unfortunate," the chubby one commented. "We'll have to dispose of him."

"Demolecularization is the best way," Giovanni put in immediately.

"Dispose of him *humanely*, I mean. It's revolting to think of taking the life of an inferior being. But he simply can't remain in this fourspace any longer, not if he Knows."

"But I *don't* know!" Al groaned. "I couldn't be any more mixed-up if I tried! Won't you please tell me—"

"Very well," said the pudgiest one, who seemed to be the leader. "Waldemar, tell him about Us."

Waldemar said, "You're now in the local headquarters of a secret mutant group working for the overthrow of humanity as you know it. By some accident you happened to dial our private communication exchange, MUtant 4—"

"I thought it was MUgwump 4," Al interjected.

"The code name, naturally," said Waldemar smoothly. "To continue: you channeled into our communication network. You now know too much. Your presence in this space-time nexus jeopardizes the success of our entire movement. Therefore we are forced—"

"To demolecularize—" Giovanni began.

"Forced to dispose of you," Waldemar continued sternly. "We're humane beings—most of us—and we won't do anything that would make you suffer. But you can't stay in this area of space-time. You see our point of view, of course."

Al shook his head dimly. These little potbellied men were mutants working for the overthrow of humanity? Well, he had no reason to think they were lying to him. The world was full of little potbellied men. Maybe they were all part of the secret organization, Al thought.

"Look," he said, "I didn't *want* to dial your number, get me? It was all a big accident. But I'm a fair guy. Let me get out of here and I'll keep mum about the whole thing. You can go ahead and overthrow humanity, if that's what you want to do. I promise not to interfere in any way. If you're mutants, you ought to be able to look into my mind and see that I'm sincere—"

"We have no telepathic powers," declared the chubby leader curtly. "If we had, there would be no need for a communications network in the first place. In the second place, your sincerity is not the issue. We have enemies. If you were to fall into their hands—"

"I won't say a word! Even if they stick splinters under my fingernails, I'll keep quiet!"

"No. At this stage in our campaign we can take no risks. You'll have to go. Prepare the temporal centrifuge."

Four of the little men, led by Mordecai, unveiled a complicated-looking device of the general size and shape of a concrete mixer. Waldemar and Giovanni gently shoved Al toward the machine. It came rapidly to life: dials glowed, indicator needles teetered, loud buzzes and clicks implied readiness.

Al said nervously, "What are you going to do to me?"

Waldemar explained. "This machine will hurl you forward in time. Too bad we have to rip you right out of your temporal matrix, but we've no choice. You'll be well taken care of up ahead, though. No doubt by the twenty-fifth century our kind will have taken over completely. You'll be the last of the Normals. Practically a living fossil. You'll love it. You'll be a walking museum piece."

"Assuming the machine works," Giovanni put in maliciously. "We don't really know if it does, you see."

Al gaped. They were busily strapping him to a cold copper slab in the heart of the machine. "You don't even know if it *works*?"

"Not really," Waldemar admitted. "Present theory holds that time-travel works only one way—*forward*. So we haven't been able to recover any of our test specimens and see how they reacted. Of course, they *do* vanish when the machine is turned on, so we know they must go *somewhere*."

"*Oh,*" Al said weakly.

He was trussed in thoroughly. Experimental wriggling of his right wrist showed him that. But even if he could get loose, these weird little men would only "freeze" him and put him into the machine again.

His shoulders slumped resignedly. He wondered if anyone would miss him. The Friendly Finance Corporation certainly would. But since, in a sense, it was their fault he was in this mess now, he couldn't get very upset about that. They could always sue his estate for the three hundred dollars he owed them, if his estate was worth that much.

Nobody else was going to mind the disappearance of Albert Miller from the space-time continuum, he thought dourly. His parents were dead, he hadn't seen his one sister in fifteen years, and the girl he used to know in Topeka was married and at last report had three kids.

Still and all, he rather liked 1969. He wasn't sure how he would take to the twenty-fifth century—or the twenty-fifth century to him.

"Ready for temporal discharge," Mordecai sang out.

The chubby leader peered up at Al. "We're sorry about all this, you understand. But nothing and nobody can be allowed to stand in the way of the Cause."

"Sure," Al said. "I understand."

The concrete-mixer part of the machine began to revolve, bearing Al with it as it built up tempokinetic potential. Momentum increased alarmingly. In the background Al heard an ominous droning sound that grew louder and louder, until it drowned out everything else. His head reeled. The room and its fat little mutants went blurry. He heard a *pop!* like the sound of a breaking balloon.

It was the rupturing of the space-time continuum. Al Miller went hurtling forward along the fourspace track, head first. He shut his eyes and hoped for the best.

When the dizziness stopped, he found himself sitting in the middle of an impeccably clean, faintly yielding roadway, staring up at the wheels of vehicles swishing by overhead at phenomenal speeds. After a moment or two more, he realized they were not airborne, but simply automobiles racing along an elevated roadway made of some practically invisible substance.

So the temporal centrifuge *had* worked! Al glanced around. A crowd was collecting. A couple of hundred people had formed a big circle. They were pointing and muttering. Nobody approached closer than fifty or sixty feet.

They weren't potbellied mutants. Without exception they were all straight-backed six-footers with full heads of hair. The women were tall, too. Men and women alike were dressed in a sort of tunic-like garment made of iridescent material that constantly changed colors.

A gong began to ring, rapidly peaking in volume. Al scrambled to his feet and assayed a tentative smile.

"My name's Miller. I come from 1969. Would somebody mind telling me what year this is, and—"

He was drowned out by two hundred voices screaming in terror. The crowd stampeded away, dashing madly in every direction, as if he were some ferocious monster. The gong continued to clang loudly. Cars hummed overhead. Suddenly Al saw a squat, beetle-shaped black vehicle coming toward him on the otherwise empty road. The car pulled up half a block away, the top sprang open, and a figure clad in what might have been a diver's suit—or a spacesuit—stepped out and advanced toward Al.

"Dozzinon murrifar volan," the armored figure called out.

"No speaka da lingo," Al replied. "I'm a stranger here."

To his dismay he saw the other draw something shaped like a weapon and point it at him. Al's hands shot immediately into the air. A globe of bluish light exuded from the broad nuzzle of the gun, hung suspended for a moment, and drifted toward Al. He dodged uneasily to one side, but the globe of light followed him, descended, and wrapped itself completely around him.

It was like being on the inside of a soap bubble. He could see out, though distortedly. He touched the curving side of the glove experimentally; it was resilient and springy to the touch, but his finger did not penetrate.

He noticed with some misgiving that his bubble cage was starting to drift off the ground. It trailed a rope-like extension, which the man in the spacesuit deftly grabbed and knotted to the rear bumper of his car. He drove quickly away—with Al, bobbing in his impenetrable bubble of light, tagging willy-nilly along like a caged tiger, or like a captured Gaul being dragged through the streets of Rome behind a chariot.

He got used to the irregular motion after a while, and relaxed enough to be able to study his surroundings. He was passing through a remarkably antiseptic-looking city, free from refuse and dust. Towering buildings, all bright and spankingly new-looking, shot up everywhere. People goggled at him from the safety of the pedestrian walkways as he jounced past.

After about ten minutes the car halted outside an imposing building whose facade bore the words ISTFAQ BARNOLL. Three men in spacesuits appeared from within to flank Al's captor as a kind of honor guard. Al was borne within.

He was nudged gently into a small room on the ground floor. The door rolled shut behind him and seemed to join the rest of the wall; no division line was apparent. A moment later the balloon popped open, and just in time, too; the air had been getting quite stale inside it.

Al glanced around. A square window opened in the wall and three grim-faced men peered intently at him from an adjoining cubicle. A voice from a speaker grid above Al's head said, "Murrifar althrosk?"

"Al Miller, from the twentieth century. And it wasn't my idea to come here, believe me."

"Durberal haznik? Quittimar? Dorbfenk?"

Al shrugged. "No parley-voo. Honest, I don't savvy."

His three interrogators conferred among themselves—taking what seemed to Al like the needless precaution of switching off the mike to prevent him from overhearing their deliberations. He saw one of the men leave the observation cubicle. When he returned, some five minutes later, he brought with him a tall, gloomy-looking man wearing an impressive spade-shaped beard.

The mike was turned on again. Spadebeard said rumblingly, "How be thou hight?"

"Eh?"

"An thou reck the King's tongue. I conjure thee speak!"

Al grinned. No doubt they had fetched an expert in ancient languages to talk to him. "Right language, but the wrong time. I'm from the *twentieth* century. Come forward a ways."

Spadebeard paused to change mental gears. "A thousand pardons—I mean, *sorry*. Wrong idiom. Dig me now?"

"I follow you. What year is this?"

"It is 2431. And from whence be you?"

"You don't quite have it straight, yet. But I'm from 1969."

"And how come you hither?"

"I wish I knew," Al said. "I was just trying to phone the loan company, see . . . anyway, I got involved with these little fat guys who wanted to take over the world. Mutants, they said they were. And they decided they had to get rid of me, so they bundled me into their time machine and shot me forward. So I'm here."

"A spy of the mutated ones, eh?"

"Spy? Who said anything about being a spy? Talk about jumping to conclusions! I'm—"

"You have been sent by Them to wreak mischief among us. No transparent story of yours will deceive us. You are not the first to come to our era, you know. And you will meet the same fate the others met."

Al shook his head foggily. "Look here, you're making some big mistake. I'm not a spy for anybody. And I don't want to get involved in any war between you and the mutants—"

"The war is over. The last of the mutated ones was exterminated fifty years ago."

"Okay, then. What can you fear from me? Honest, I don't want to cause any trouble. If the mutants are wiped out, how could my spying help them?"

"No action in time and space is ever absolute. In our fourspace the mutants are eradicated—but they lurk elsewhere, waiting for their chance to enter and spread destruction."

Al's brain was swimming. "Okay, let that pass. But I'm *not* a spy. I just want to be left alone. Let me settle down here somewhere—put me on probation—show me the ropes, stake me to a few credits, or whatever you use for money here. I won't make any trouble."

"Your body teems with microorganisms of disease long since extinct in this world. Only the fact that we were able to confine you in a force-bubble almost as soon as you arrived here saved us from a terrible epidemic of ancient diseases."

"A couple of injections, that's all, and you can kill any bacteria on me," Al pleaded. "You're advanced people. You ought to be able to do a simple thing like that."

"And then there is the matter of your genetic structure," Spadebeard continued inexorably. "You bear genes long since eliminated from humanity as undesirable. Permitting you to remain here, breeding uncontrollably, would introduce unutterable confusion. Perhaps you carry latently the same mutant strain that cost humanity so many centuries of bloodshed!"

"No," Al protested. "Look at me. I'm six feet tall, no potbelly, a full head of hair—"

"The gene is recessive. But it crops up unexpectedly."

"I solemnly promise to control my breeding," Al declared. "I won't run around scattering my genes all over your shiny new world. That's a promise."

"Your appeal is rejected," came the inflexible reply.

Al shrugged. He knew when he was beaten. "Okay," he said wearily. "I didn't want to live in your damn century anyway. When's the execution?"

"*Execution?*" Spadebeard looked stunned. "The twentieth-century referent—yes, it is! Dove's whiskers, do you think we would—would actually—"

He couldn't get the word out. Al supplied it.

"Put me to death?"

Spadebeard's expression was sickly. He looked ready to retch. Al heard him mutter vehemently to his companions in the observation cubicle: "Gonnim def larrimog! Egfar!"

"Murrifar althrosk," suggested one of his companions.

Spadebeard, evidently reassured, nodded. He said to Al, "No doubt a barbarian like yourself *would* expect to be—to be made dead." Gulping, he went gamely on. "We have no such vindictive intention."

"Well, what *are* you going to do to me?"

"Send you across the timeline to a world where your friends the mutated ones reign supreme," Spadebeard replied. "It's the least we can do for you, spy."

The hidden door of his cell puckered open. Another space-suited figure entered, pointed a gun, and discharged a blob of blue light that drifted toward Al and rapidly englobed him. He was drawn by the trailing end out into a corridor.

It hadn't been a very sociable reception, here in the twenty-fifth Century, he thought as he was tugged along the hallway. In a way, he couldn't blame them. A time-traveler from the past was bound to be laden down with all sorts of germs. They couldn't risk letting him run around *breathing* at everybody. No wonder that crowd of onlookers had panicked when he opened his mouth to speak to them.

The other business, though, that of his being a spy for the mutants—he couldn't figure that out at all. If the mutants had been wiped out fifty years ago, why worry about spies now? At least his species had managed to defeat the underground organization of potbellied little men. That was comforting. He wished he could get back to 1969 if only to snap his fingers in their jowly faces and tell them that all their sinister scheming was going to come to nothing.

Where was he heading now? Spadebeard had said, *Across the timeline to a world where the mutated ones reign supreme.* Whatever across the timeline meant, Al thought.

He was ushered into an impressive laboratory room and, bubble and all, was thrust into the waiting clasps of something that looked depressingly like an electric chair. Brisk technicians bustled around, throwing switches and checking connections.

Al glanced appealingly at Spadebeard. "Will you tell me what's going on?"

"It is very difficult to express it in medieval terms," the linguist said. "The device makes us of dollibar force to transmit you through an inverse dormin vector—do I make myself clear?"

"Not very."

"Unhelpable. But you understand the concept of parallel continua at least, of course."

"No."

"Does it mean anything to you if I say that you'll be shunted across the spokes of the time-wheel to a totality that is simultaneously parallel and tangent to our fourspace?"

"I get the general idea," Al said dubiously, though all he was really getting was a headache. "You might as well start shunting me, I suppose."

Spadebeard nodded and turned to a technician. "Vorstrar althrosk," he commanded.

"Murrifar."

The technician grabbed an immense toggle-switch with both hands and groaningly dragged it shut. Al heard a brief shine of closing relays. Then darkness surrounded him.

Once again he found himself on a city street. But the pavement was cracked and buckled, and grass blades shot up through the neglected concrete.

A dry voice said, "All right, you. Don't sprawl there like a ninny. Get up and come along."

Al peered doubtfully up into the snout of a fair-sized pistol of enormous caliber. It was held by a short, fat, bald-headed man. Four identical companions stood near him with arms folded. They all looked very much like Mordecai, Waldemar, Giovanni, and the rest, except that these mutants were decked out in futuristic-looking costumes bright with flashy gold trim and rocketship insignia.

Al put up his hands. "Where am I?" he asked hesitantly.

"Earth, of course. You've just come through a dimensional gateway from the continuum of the Normals. Come along, spy. Into the van."

"But I'm *not* a spy," Al mumbled protestingly, as the five little men bundled him into a blue-and-red car the size of a small yacht. "At least, I'm not spying on *you*. I mean—"

"Save the explanations for the Overlord," was the curt instruction.

Al huddled miserably cramped between two vigilant mutants, while the others sat behind him. The van moved seemingly of its own volition, and at an enormous rate. A mutant power, Al thought. After a while he said, "Could you at least tell me what year this is?"

"It is 2431," snapped the mutant to his left.

"But that's the same year it was over *there*."

"Of course. What did you expect?"

The question floored Al. He was silent for perhaps half a mile more. Since the van had no windows, he stared morosely at his feet. Finally he asked, "How come you aren't afraid of catching my germs, then? Over back of—ah—the dimensional gateway, they kept me cooped up in a force-field all the time so I wouldn't contaminate them. But you go right ahead breathing the same air I do."

"Do you think we fear the germs of a Normal, spy?" sneered the mutant at Al's right. "You forget that we're a superior race."

Al nodded. "Yes. I forgot about that."

The van halted suddenly and the mutant police hustled Al out, past a crowd of peering little fat men and women, and into a colossal dome of a building whose exterior was covered completely with faceted green glass. The effect was one of massive ugliness.

They ushered him into a sort of throne room presided over by a mutant fatter than the rest. The policeman gripping Al's right arm hissed, "Bow when you enter the presence of the Overlord."

Al wasn't minded to argue. He dropped to his knees along with the others. A booming voice from above rang out, "What have you brought me today?"

"A spy, your nobility."

"Another? Rise, spy."

Al rose. "Begging your nobility's pardon, I'd like to put in a word or two on my own behalf—"

"Silence!" the Overlord roared.

Al closed his mouth. The mutant drew himself up to his full height, about five feet one, and said, "The Normals have sent you across the dimensional gulf to spy on us."

"No, your nobility. They were afraid I'd spy on *them*, so they tossed me over here. I'm from the year 1969, you see." Briefly, he explained everything, beginning with the bollixed phone call and ending with his capture by the Overlord's men a short while ago.

The Overlord looked skeptical. "It is well known that the Normals plan to cross the dimensional gulf from their phantom world to this, the real one, and invade our civilization. You're but the latest of their advance scouts. Admit it!"

"Sorry, your nobility, but I'm not. On the other side they told me I was a spy from 1969, and now you say I'm a spy from the other dimension. But I tell you—"

"Enough!" the mutant leader thundered. "Take him away. Place him in custody. We shall decide his fate later!"

Someone else already occupied the cell into which Al was thrust. He was a lanky, sad-faced Normal who slouched forward to shake hands once the door had clanged shut.

"Thurizad manifosk," he said.

"Sorry. I don't speak that language," said Al.

The other grinned. "I understand. All right: greetings. I'm Darren Phelp. Are you a spy too?"

"No, dammit!" Al snapped. Then: "Sorry. Didn't mean to take it out on you. My name's Al Miller. Are you a native of this place?"

"Me? Dove's whiskers, what a sense of humor! Of course I'm not a native! You know as well as I do that there aren't any Normals left in this fourspace continuum."

"None at all?"

"Hasn't been one born here in centuries," Phelp said. "But you're just joking, eh? You're from Baileffod's outfit, I suppose."

"Who?"

"Baileffod. *Baileffod!* You mean you aren't? Then you must be from Higher Up!" Phelp thrust his hands sideways in some kind of gesture of respect. "Penguin's paws, Excellency, I apologize. I should have seen at once—"

"No, I'm not from your organization at all," Al said. "I don't know what you're talking about, really."

Phelp smiled cunningly. "Of *course*, Excellency! I understand completely."

"Cut that out! Why doesn't anyone ever believe me? I'm not from Baileffod and I'm not from Higher Up. I come from 1969. Do you hear me, 1969? And that's the truth."

Phelp's eyes went wide. "From the *past?*"

Al nodded. "I stumbled into the mutants in 1969 and they threw me five centuries ahead to get rid of me. Only when I arrived, I wasn't welcome, so I was shipped across the dimensional whatzis to here. Everyone thinks I'm a spy, wherever I go. What are *you* doing here?"

Phelp smiled. "Why, I *am* a spy."

"From 2431?"

"Naturally. We have to keep tabs on the mutants somehow. I came through the gateway wearing an invisibility shield, but it popped an ultrone and I vizzed out. They jugged me last month, and I suppose I'm here for keeps."

Al rubbed thumbs tiredly against his eyeballs. "Wait a minute—how come you speak my language? On the other side they had to get a linguistics expert to talk to me."

"All spies are trained to talk English, stupid. That's the language the mutants speak here. In the real world we speak Vorkish, naturally. It's the language developed by Normals for communication during the Mutant Wars. Your 'linguistics expert' was probably one of our top spies."

"And over here the mutants have won?"

"Completely. Three hundred years ago, in this continuum, the mutants developed a two-way time machine that enabled them to go back and forth, eliminating Normal leaders before they were born. Whereas in our world, the *real* world, two-way time travel is impossible. That's where the continuum split begins. We Normals fought a grim war of extermination against the mutants in our fourspace and finally wiped them out, despite their superior mental powers, in 2390. Clear?"

"More or less." Rather less than more, Al added privately. "So there are only mutants in this world, and only Normals in your world."

"Exactly."

"And you're a spy from the other side."

"You've got it now! You see, even though strictly speaking this world is only a phantom, it's got some pretty real characteristics. For instance, if the mutants killed you here, you'd be dead. Permanently. So there's a lot of rivalry across the gateway; the mutants are always scheming to invade us, and vice versa. Confidentially, I don't think anything will ever come of all the scheming."

"You don't?"

"Nah," Phelp said. "The way things stand now, each side has a perfectly good enemy just beyond reach. But actually going to war would be messy, while relaxing our guard and slipping into peace would foul up our economy. So we keep sending spies back and forth, and prepare for war. It's a nice system, except when you happen to get caught, like me."

"What'll happen to you?"

Phelp shrugged. "They may let me rot here for a few decades. Or they might decide to condition me and send me back as a spy for *them*. Tiger tails, who knows?"

"Would you change sides like that?"

"I wouldn't have any choice—not after I was conditioned," Phelp said. "But I don't worry much about it. It's a risk I knew about when I signed on for spy duty."

Al shuddered. It was beyond him how someone could *voluntarily* let himself get involved in this game of dimension-shifting and mutant-battling. But it takes all sorts to make a continuum, he decided.

Half an hour later three rotund mutant police came to fetch

him. They marched him downstairs and into a bare, ugly little room where a battery of interrogators quizzed him for better than an hour. He stuck to his story, throughout everything, until at last they indicated they were through with him. He spent the next two hours in a drafty cell, by himself, until finally a gaudily robed mutant unlocked the door and said, "The Overlord wishes to see you."

The Overlord looked worried. He leaned forward on his throne, fist digging into his fleshy chin. In his booming voice—Al realized suddenly that it was artfically amplified—the Overlord rumbled, "Miller, you're a *problem*."

"I'm sorry, your nobil——"

"*Quiet!* I'll do the talking."

Al did not reply.

The Overlord went on, "We've checked your story inside and out, and confirmed it with one of our spies on the other side of the gate. You really *are* from 1969, or thereabouts. What can we do with you? Generally speaking, when we catch a Normal snooping around here, we psychocondition him and send him back across the gateway to spy for us. But we can't do that to you, because you don't belong on the other side, and they've already tossed you out once. On the other hand, we can't keep you here, maintaining you forever at state expense. And it wouldn't be civilized to kill you, would it?"

"No, your nobil——"

"*Silence!*"

Al gulped. The Overlord glowered at him and continued thinking out loud. "I suppose we could perform experiments on you, though. You must be a walking laboratory of Normal microorganisms that we could synthesize and fire through the gateway when we invade their fourspace. Yes, by the Grome, then you'd be useful to our cause! Zechariah?"

"Yes, Nobility?" A ribbon-bedecked guardsman snapped to attention.

"Take this Normal to the Biological Laboratories for examination. I'll have further instructions as soon as—"

Al heard a peculiar whanging noise from the back of the throne room. The Overlord appeared to freeze on his throne. Turning, Al saw a band of determined-looking Normals come bursting in, led by Darren Phelp.

"*There* you are!" Phelp cried. "I've been looking all over for you!" He was waving a peculiar needle-nozzled gun.

"What's going on?" Al asked.

Phelp grinned. "The Invasion! It came, after all! Our troops are pouring through the gateway armed with these freezer guns. They immobilize any mutant who gets in the way of the field."

"When—when did all this happen?"

"It started two hours ago. We've captured the entire city! Come on, will you? Whiskers, there's no time to waste!"

"Where am I supposed to go?"

Phelp smiled. "To the nearest dimensional lab, of course. We're going to send you back home."

A dozen triumphant Normals stood in a tense knot around Al in the laboratory. From outside came the sound of jubilant singing. The Invasion was a howling success.

As Phelp had explained it, the victory was due to the recent invention of a kind of time-barrier projector. The projector had cut off all contact between the mutant world and its own future, preventing time-traveling mutant scouts from getting back to 2431 with news of the Invasion. Thus two-way travel, the great mutant advantage, was nullified, and the success of the surprise attack was made possible.

Al listened to this explanation with minimal interest. He barely understood every third word, and, in any event, his main concern was in getting home.

He was strapped into a streamlined and much modified version of the temporal centrifuge that had originally hurled him into 2431. Phelp explained things to him.

"You see here, we set the machine for 1969. What day was it when you left?"

"Ah—October ten. Around three thirty in the afternoon."

"Make the setting, Frozz." Phelp nodded. "You'll be shunted back along the time-line. Of course, you'll land in this continuum, since in our world there's no such thing as pastward time travel. But once you reach your own time, all you do is activate this small transdimensional generator, and you'll be hurled across safe and sound into the very day you left, in your own fourspace."

"You can't know how much I appreciate all this," Al said warmly. He felt a pleasant glow of love for all mankind, for the first time since his unhappy phone call. At last someone was taking sympathetic interest in his plight. At last, he was on his way home, back to the relative sanity of 1969, where he could start forgetting this entire nightmarish jaunt. Mutants and Normals and spies and time machines—

"You'd better get going," Phelp said. "We have to get the occupation under way here."

"Sure," Al agreed. "Don't let me hold you up. I can't wait to get going—no offense intended."

"And remember—soon as your surroundings look familiar, jab the activator button on this generator. Otherwise you'll slither into an interspace where we couldn't answer for the consequences."

Al nodded tensely. "I won't forget."

"I hope not. Ready?"

"Ready."

Someone threw a switch. Al began to spin. He heard the popping sound that was the rupturing of the temporal matrix. Like a cork shot from a champagne bottle, Al arched out backward through time, heading for 1969.

He woke in his own room on Twenty-third Street. His head hurt. His mind was full of phrases like temporal centrifuge and transdimensional generator.

He picked himself off the floor and rubbed his head.

Wow, he thought. It must have been a sudden fainting spell. And now his head was full of nonsense.

Going to the sideboard, he pulled out the half-empty bourbon bottle and measured off a few fingers' worth. After the drink, his nerves felt steadier. His mind was still cluttered with inexplicable thoughts and images. Sinister little fat men and complex machines, gleaming roadways and men in fancy tunics.

A bad dream, he thought.

Then he remembered. It wasn't any dream. He had actually taken the round trip into 2431, returning by way of some other continuum. He had pressed the generator button at the proper time, and now here he was, safe and sound. No longer the football of a bunch of different factions. Home in his own snug little fourspace, or whatever it was.

He frowned. He recalled that Mordecai had severed the telephone wire. But the phone looked intact now. Maybe it had been fixed while he was gone. He picked it up. Unless he got that loan extension today, he was cooked.

There was no need for him to look up the number of the Friendly Finance Corporation; he knew it well enough. He began to dial. MUrray Hill 4—

The receiver clicked queerly. A voice said, "Come in, Operator Nine. Operator Nine, do you read me?"

Al's jaw sagged in horror. This is where I came in, he thought wildly. He struggled to put down the phone. But his muscles would not respond. It would be easier to bend the sun in its orbit than to break the path of the continuum. He heard his own voice say, "I didn't want the operator. There must be something wrong with my phone if—"

"Just a minute. Who *are* you?"

Al fought to break the contact. But he was hemmed away in a small corner of his mind while his voice went on, "I ought to ask *you* that. What are you doing on the other end of my phone, anyway? I hadn't even finished dialing. I got as far as MU-4 and—"

Inwardly Al wanted to scream. No scream would come. In this continuum the past (his future) was immutable. He was caught on the track, and there was no escape. None whatever. And, he realized glumly, there never would be.

SECRET RIDER

MARTA RANDALL

Marta Randall is a young California writer whose stories and novels have won her increasing praise in the past few years. She has published two books, Islands *and* A City in the North; *and among her best shorter works is this crisp, taut, and dizzying tale of a quest that zigzags across time.*

> "Foundering between eternity and time,
> we are amphibians and must accept the fact."
> —ALDOUS HUXLEY, from *Theme and Variations*

I

She had followed him across the galaxy.
Twice.
Always arriving the barest moment too late, always just behind the jet that left, the ship that sailed, the tauship that taued the day before, carrying him with it. On Gardenia they told her he had gone to witness the Rites of the Resurrected; she flew over the face of the globe, pushing the sled to its limits above the checkerboard jungle, arriving in time to see the thin contrails of his jets leaving the Awakening Place toward the Port. Followed him to Asperity, to Quintesme, to Jakob's World, to New Aqaba, where she thought she saw him entering a sky-blue mosque. But, again, she was wrong. To Nineveh Down. To

Poltergeist. To Jason's Lift. Past stars as yet unnamed, booking passage on the quickest, the fleetest, second-guessing his guessing mind.

She had something of his, sewn under the skin of her thigh. Kept warm and secret, although it demanded neither. Perhaps he no longer needed it, certainly had forgotten it might have existed, but she had it and wanted to give it to him. Besides, she loved him.

On Murphy's Landing she shared a hotel with him, unbeknownst to either of them. Had arrived, body-time at sleepless dawn in the bright morning light; had registered, slept, woke at planet-noon to ask the questions she had been too tired to ask before, discovered he had just, barely, left. And no room on the ship for her. Didn't weep, but wanted to. What use?

Back home, her children grew older and younger, cities failed and flourished, she herself died many times. On Asperity at 1852 Earth Time, on Jason's Lift at 3042 E.T., on Soft Conception at 1153 E.T.; Constantinople toppled while she argued with border guards, New Jerusalem rose to the stars as she slept exhausted in the arms of a stranger on Endgame II.

II

Tau travel does not necessarily do odd things to time, nor is it true to say that time does odd things during tau travel. Were tau a linear projection, a straight line running alongside the other straight and infinite lines of the universe, it would be possible to say that there is some correlation between the Y of tau and the Z of time, it would be possible to perceive a correspondence and arrive at a formula for controlling tau-shift. But tau doesn't work that way. Leave Parnell for Ararat and when you arrive Parnell may not have been discovered, might have centuried to dust in the wake of your passing. Ararat, clear in the telescopes of Parnell, might be still a formless cloud shivering in the pull of gravity's shaping. Tau takes you to a place, but the time is of its own choosing, and random. And so the terminals, the gaping jaws that connect real space and tau space; time-machines, capable of plucking a ship from tau and sending it into reality precisely at the time demanded. Which may or may not be seven months' time from the beginning of a seven months' journey. Why dismiss the possibilities of a burnt planet that once was green, simply because it met its death four thousand years before the Terran seas were formed? Or because it had not yet been born, not in real-space? Humanity, not content with having the universe for a playground, delved into past and future, and lost itself amid the ages of the stars.

III

She lost the trail on Nueva Azteca, spent hours and days tracking those who had served him or seen him during his brief stay on the pyramid planet. A porter at the hotel had overheard his plans to book for Leman, but the port records did not carry his name for that destination; the Colonial Administrator's office offered the information that he had requested a visa-stamp for Hell's Outpost but, again, there was no record of his departure.

She got drunk on heavy beer and sobered in steam showers, accepted an invitation to ColAd's yearly celebration and spent the evening curled in a corner, hopelessly scanning the tri-dims of Galactic Central that floated through the noise and scents of the transparent room. Queried every shipping company serving the planet and sat back to await the answers to her questions. They came in over the next planet-months; no, and no, and not since five years back and then in a completely different sector. She swam in the dark red waters of the inland sea and safaried across the endless plains that girdled the planet at the equator. Cupped her hand over her thigh in the night and never considered going home.

IV

He had been with her during the birth of her daughter, floating weightless with her in the labor sphere while her body paced through the rhythms of childbirth. Had kept her mind on the hypnotic convolutions when she tended to wander, helping her pulse love and warmth toward the tiny soul working its way from her body and, finally, had taken the wrinkled, squalling infant from the doctors and placed it in her arms, sharing her joy.

She had feared, during those last weeks before delivery, that the coming changes would also change their love, that in some manner the intensity would dissipate the fires of their first loving, three months back. Yet he had accepted this doubling of herself, as he had accepted her rounded belly, with a fierce tenderness that in its own fashion equaled the depthlessness of her own love.

He left Interplanetary and took assignments closer to Terra; she refused an engineering assignment that would have taken her halfway across the sector and contented herself with minor jumps through Terra End. They calculated their comings together carefully, always reappearing on Terra a week planet-time after they had left. It didn't matter that their bio-ages shifted, that each one was, alternately, older and then younger than the other. Accept off-planet jobs and one had to accept the mismatch of planet-time and bio-age. They loved, and bio-time had little to do with that.

But the time-shifts made it harder to note other differences, harder to decide which were the natural changes of age and which were the unnatural transmutations of illness.

Until the changes became very clear, and now it was her turn to sit nervous in waiting areas, to help him through the tests, to await not the delivery of a child but the delivery of a verdict, an opinion, an identification. First with hope, then with faith, through his growing desperation. Waiting.

Two years had passed for her daughter, seven for herself, six for him, when they told her that he would have to die.

V

The night the last negative answer arrived, she pulled a dark clingsuit over her slim body and ventured into the Aztecan evening to drink, smoke, ingest, sniff, swirl, unsync—all, if possible, simultaneously. Started high and moved lower during the course of the night, from the elegant dignity of a crystalline cube that floated over the apex of the largest pyramid to an expensive tourist club clinging to the sides of a seacliff to a raucous gathering at the home of the Attaché for Sensory Importation to a neighborhood saloon where they threw her out after five Bitter Centauris. Found herself, at dawn, half draped over a table at SeaCave, a spacer's bar at the bottom of the bay where she had been once before during her quest, but not in her present condition. Peered at the double-imaged, blasted face across from her and asked her usual question.

"Yeah, I know the knocker," the harsh voice replied. She extracted the words from the stoneapple haze, pulled herself nearly upright and forced the double images to resolve into one.

"When?"

" 'Bout three runs ago. Booked passage from here to Augustine. Funny knocker, came on board something unusual." The voice paused.

"Want another drink?" she asked.

"Naw, I'm up enough."

"Food?"

"Cash," he suggested.

"Cash. Okay. How much?"

"How much do you want to know?"

She considered, then excused herself, found the dispos and cleaned her stomach, bought a sobor from the vending machine and pressed the vial to her arm, felt the coolness of rationality return. Made her way back to the bar and sat beside her informant.

The blasted face turned toward her and now, without the deceptive veils of high, she could see the spaceburns and fightburns, the scars where an eye had been replaced with a maximum of haste and a minimum of skill. The hand wrapped around the vibraglass had thick, splayed fingers, some one joint long, some two, none of them whole. Rivers and streams of scars flowed down his neck and under the top of his battered tunic, emerged again to run down his forearms and fingers.

"Pretty, ain't I?" the spacer asked, grinning. There was no telling where the scars ended and his lips began.

"Why don't you . . ."

"Get fixed? Why bother? Not bad enough yet, give me another run or so and it'll be due for a clean-up, then I'll just bash it up again." The spacer shrugged.

"Want another drink?" she asked.

"And cash?"

"Sure. How much do you know?"

"How much've you got?"

"I want to know what you meant by boarding unusually."

"Ten skims."

"Skims?"

"Units, graffs, get me?"

She pulled ten from her hip pouch and put it on the table, covering it with her hand.

"Talk."

"Well, it was about five to lift-off . . ."

"To Augustine?"

"Yeah."

"Augustine when?"

"Five skims."

"Later."

"Your chips, lady. So everything was pretty much battered down, we had the hoppers in gear and were just about to cut cords when this knocker comes sprinting over from Main and through the cord. Seems there was a cancel-out about half hour before lift-off and this knocker came in on stand-by, just made it to the port on time."

"Go on."

"That's ten skims' worth."

"The hell it is. There's nothing unusual about someone boarding late, there's always one."

The spacer shrugged. She lifted her free hand and ordered a

DoubleTaker for him, a glass of innocuous JelWatr for herself. The drinks arrived and the floating tray hovered for a moment while she pressed her thumb to the plate. The empty glasses winked out, the transparent cover of the tray snicked down and the tray floated away.

"You gonna give me the ten?"

"If you finish giving me ten's worth."

Their eyes met over the radiant blackness of the table, then he dropped his glance and poured the 'Taker down his throat.

"Okay, lady. What was funny was he wore the wrong name."

She pushed the ten to him and replaced it with a five.

"Augustine when?"

"Twenty-five odd, seven down."

"Name?"

He watched her add another five to the one already under her palm.

"Called himself Johan Ab'naua, but before we reached the grab he, uh, asked me to get rid of some old tags for him. They said 'John Albion.'"

She pushed the money to him, sat back, finished her drink.

The next day she booked passage for Augustine, twenty-five odd, seven down.

When she got there, he was dead.

VI

Or, at any rate, Johan Ab'naua was dead. The body was prepared for burial, but she bribed one of the morgue attendants to let her see. Tension twisted within her as the tall women led her down to the cold vaults, swung open the heavy door and ushered her into a room with numbered doors lining the sides. Her hand drifted down to rest lightly on her thigh as the attendant selected the appropriate door, opened it, and the transparent rectangle floated into the room.

The coroner's report, 'hezed to the end of the rectangle, was quite thorough. It talked about traces of radiation damage and talked about traces of chemicals found in the body, mentioned half a dozen, each one fatal in the proper amount. Talked about an excess of water in the tissues and speculated on immersion before the deceased deceased. Considered the fusion burns, speculated on the possibility that weapons were used to put the deceased out of the misery undoubtedly caused by the above-stated factors, or, perhaps, to disfigure the departed beyond recognition. Or to cover the radiation, and the poison, and the water. Mentioned the difficulty of effecting a true recognition from the remains and boasted of positive identification achieved through thorough and painstaking work. The amorphous mass in the glass coffin, the coroner's report insisted, was all that remained of Johan Ab'naua.

She glanced inside the rectangle quickly, then thanked the attendant, passed over the balance of the bribe and returned to her hotel.

VII

Was he dead because she hadn't reached him, or dead because she had?

Their times, she knew, had crossed before. Even before he had journeyed out so far, even before she had tucked a secret in her thigh and followed him, their various whens had crossed and recrossed—he older and she younger, or she older and he younger, backward, forward. It was possible that at some future biological date she would meet him before his death, would give him the ampule stitched beneath the skin of her leg. His death was no reason to end the quest. It was, simply, a matter of timing.

Somewhen, curling through the intricacies of tau, John/Johan still lived. Somewhen on this very planet he lived, but that past was closed to her as completely as it would have been without tau. There are laws that maintain the continuity of planet-time, strictly enforced regulations proscribing visits to a planet at any time previous to one's first planet-time visit, that forbid jumping on-planet itself. How else to cope with the ensuing chaos, how maintain a measured sanity in the face of life when tomorrow is last week and yesterday happens next year, when your great-great-great grandfather drops in for a drink ten minutes before the arrival of your current lover, who hasn't been born yet? They try to enforce planet-time laws as strictly as the universe enforces the laws of gravity, as rigorously as light follows the dictates of real-space. Or she would have leaped backward after that first near-miss, countless planetfalls ago; would leap back now, into John's Augustine life.

Yet, had one the time, the resources, the contacts, the courage, there was a way to circumvent the laws. Name changes, print changes, the subtle individualities of the body rearranged, and one could slip by the guardians of time, revisit the past of one's present. John must have done it. Otherwise, why the change of name? Why the end of the trail on Nueva Azteca, why the misnamed body lying frozen in the morgue?

She could not duplicate his feat. She lacked the resources, the contacts, perhaps even the courage to have her life changed. And so, again, it came to this: a matter of timing.

She rose from her bed, wrapped herself in warmth and went to trace his death through the glittering austerity of the city.

VIII

Augustine is a sovereign nation, a chartered member of the Union of All Worlds, and consequently information was harder to obtain than it had been from the various ColAd agencies on Nueva Azteca. His effects? In storage, where they would remain for seven years unless claimed by a relative. Could she, perhaps, prove relationship with Johan Ab'naua? No, not with Johan. Sorry. After seven years the effects will be destroyed. She looked at the pinched, bureaucratic face before her and dismissed the idea of bribery.

She had no better luck at the port. The passenger lists were closed, confidential. But the clerk was sympathetic and suggested the files of the local newsfax, the public lists of entry and exit taken not from the port but from customs. So she booked time on the public computer and keyed in her request.

Johan Ab'naua had arrived on Augustine ten weeks before. Had been discovered dead in a back alley in Port Sector four days ago—a small story, that. Violent deaths in any port sector are far from a rarity. A holo from his passport accompanied the story, a chip taken from the main crystal, for the resolution was fuzzy, the colors off. But she recognized John Albion's face behind the subtle changes. So.

She thumbed the connection closed and went out to wander the city.

IX

They had tried to build Augustine austere, straight, square, grim, but the planet itself defeated them. The world's basic stone was a refractive crystal, hard and shimmering, and only it would stand up to use as a building material. The architecture of the city was all cubes and rectangles—small, severe windows and disapproving right angles, built of glimmering, color-changing crystals that reflected the flowing of wind and temperature, turned the monastic blocks into the unexpected wonders of a drug dream. The citizens strode purposefully amid these hulking fantasies, dressed close and severely, grim of eye and lip. She hurried past them, knowing that their sour glances were not for her alone but for the entire universe that, in creating their planet, had played them such a dirty trick.

As she wandered away from the city proper and more deeply into Port Sector, the texture of the city changed. The buildings were now covered with layers of grime, the filth bringing them closer to the ideal of the founding fathers than the more respectable, and clean, parts of the city. Yet the people were less grim here, the spacers decked in the usual collection of charms and artifacts, no two alike and not a one drab. She moved among spacers and whores and drug pushers, asking questions, and at last stood in a small alley that ran between a block of tenements.

Nothing there, of course. Nothing to tell her how or when or even where he had met his death on the oil-streaked pavement.

She walked the alley twice, staring so intently that she felt intimate with each small crevice and corner, each pile and heap, each crack and discoloration. She found no answers to her silent questions; the walls kept their counsel, and after a while she left.

X

Evening of the thirty-hour day was beginning and numerous establishments in Port Sector had their glaring come-ons already lit. She wandered past, unseeing, her dark hair tumbling over the neck of her suit, reflecting back the lights spilled from open doors.

"Hey, spacer, wanna night?"

"Gimme some, will you?"

"Lousy knocker!"

"Lady!"

"It'll cost you, junk."

"Hey, lady!"

"Jump it, jump it, jump it!"

"Lady, wait up!"

She felt a heavy hand on her arm and raised her eyes. The spacer beside her was unfamiliar.

"Yes?"

"Hey, don't you remember me?"

She looked more carefully. The man had never been good-looking, but his face was smooth, his eyes clear and as yet unreddened by the night. Coils of orange hair, thick eyebrows, ears decked with small, mismatched cascades of jewels, body draped in iridescent shamskin. She shook her head.

"Oh, yeah, I got cleaned up. You asked me about some knocker, back on Nueva Azteca, remember?"

"Oh. Yes."

"Find him?"

"Sort of. He's dead."

"Care." The spacer raised an eyebrow. "Matter?"

"Yes, it matters."

"Care. Here, I'll stick you a drink. I need one."

She shrugged and he guided her into a dim bar, snapped his fingers for a tray as they sat behind a grid.

"You wanna JelWatr?"

She shook her head. "Whatever."

"Okay. Two Tri-levels," he told the tray, and they sat in silence until the drinks arrived. The spacer thrust his thumb at the printbox, grinned as the green panel flashed, and turned to her.

"Got paid," he explained. "You bruised?"

"I suppose."

"So goes."

She shook herself from her lethargy and glanced up at him. "How'd you get cleaned up so fast?"

"Went up to Sal, got it done in time for my next run out."

"Sal?"

"Salsipuedes. Oh, you're a knocker. You know about time regs and all that? Right. Well, you can't always get enough spacers for a run in the start port, 'cause some of em's been to the stop port up the line, see? So most ships stop at a Salsipuedes just off orbit and pick up crew, then drop them off at another Sal before the stop port. Lots of spacers get stuck that way, 'specially old ones that work just one sector and have their times so screwed up that there's no when they haven't been up the line anywhere."

"So how long did the clean-up take?"

" 'Bout a standard year. I, uh, jumped."

"Jumped?"

"Yeah, there's no time regs on a Sal. You just gotta watch out you don't meet yourself, if you're the superstitious type. Lots of spacers don't care, though. Last time up there was one old junker sitting in the lounge talking with five others of himself. Me, I don't want to know what's going to happen. Can't change it, anyway."

She felt the first level of the drink tickling at her mind and pushed the low, sweet euphoria aside.

"Look, can a . . . a knocker spend time on a Sal?"

"Yeah, sometimes. Hey, drink, you're not down to second level yet."

She raised the vibraglass to her lips and drained off the second level. It flowed down her throat like liquid stars and she felt dizzy as it hit her stomach.

"Can a knocker jump around at a Sal?"

"Maybe." His eyes narrowed and he tugged at one earring.

She considered the remaining liquid in her drink, slowly swirling it against the invisible sides of the glass.

"Look, I want to know how to get on a Sal and how to jump around once I get there."

The spacer grunted noncommitally, keeping his eyes on her.

"How much'll it cost me?"

"You alone tonight?"

She met his eyes, paused, finished her drink. And nodded.

XI

"This all of it, knocker?"

"It's all I know. From Terra to Neuhafen, to Gardenia, to Asperity, to Quintesme and the radiation labs. To Jakob's World, to New Aqaba, to Nineveh Down for the baths. To Poltergeist, to Jason's Lift, to Endgame II, to Murphy's Landing. To Nueva Azteca, to Augustine. These flights, here, these times, these ships."

"Okay, gimme another cup of that stuff. Now look, here's your sticker. All these jumps, here, they're long hops, five lights or more, see? You book for one of those, you've got to be cleared before you leave the start port. Too much trouble with knockers who make it to stop port, and then the company discovers that they've been there before, up the line, and can't afford the passage back, see? So they check you out before lift-off and save themselves the trouble. And since you *followed* him along the line, you might as well count these hops out."

"Couldn't I get on board as a spacer? They're dropped off on Sals after long hops, aren't they?"

"Yeah, sure, but look, knocker. See the band, here? It's my registry, my license. Implanted when I finished training. No way to forge one of those. Seems like you'll have to try it here, between Azteca and Augustine."

"But that's so close . . ."

"It's the only way, knocker. Sorry."

XII

The sack vibrated gently against her shoulder as she stood by the port at the jump station, watching the tau-ship move ponderously into the coil. The huge bulk slid between the heavy, curving bars, jockeyed the final humps of its tail section into place, and paused. Then it began to shimmer, so softly at first that she was not sure whether the shivering was within her mind, her eyes, rather than in the resting ship. The shimmering coalesced, expanded, sent tendrils of change over the innumerable curves and bumps of the ship. Light spilled through the bends of the coil at odd angles and odder wavelengths, a flow of molten crystals, an agglomeration of colors, a sudden transparency that wavered, disappeared, re-emerged larger than before, grew to cover the magical creation within the coils, and the ship vanished, the gaudy display cut off as abruptly as if someone had thrown a master switch and plunged the show in darkness. She shut her eyes, opened them, stared at the inert and empty coil, where not the least iridescence remained to mark the passing of the ship from one time to another. From on board ship, she remembered, it was the coil that shimmered and restablished as the translation through time took place, the universe that shook and was again steady. But nothing matched the display as seen from the jump station.

She stood alone at the receiving lock, the only one to disembark at Azteca Sal. The bursar had been furious because of her, aggrieved that her previous presence on Nueva Azteca had marred an otherwise smooth flight; had raged and stormed into her cabin, waving the GalCentral faxsheets and cursing. She had shrugged, forfeited the remainder of her passage as a result of her "carelessness" and stepped into the shuttle to the Sal without a backward glance.

The corridor stretching from the lock area toward the heart of Salsipuedes was bleak and unmarked, made no echo in response to her footsteps as she walked its length. It angled to the right and opened into an empty, ovoid room. She walked to a semiopaque shutter set into a curving wall and rapped impatiently.

"Oh, yeah, hang it," said a voice and the window sphinctered open. "Right, you're off the *Hellion*, bursar called. Want a bunk?"

"I want to jump, fourteen even, two down."

"Can't, not for another week. We've got too much coming through, can't take energy to hop a knocker around. Bunk in G'll cost you ten, private sixteen. Private? Right, level H, section four, back two. One week, okay."

She pressed her thumb against the plate and turned to go, code key in her hand.

"Hey, knocker!"

"Yes?"

"Thumb's okay here, but it won't buy you anything else on Sal."

"I know."

Her room was a bleak cube with a bunk, a clean-unit and one chair. She stowed her gear and, following the remembered words of the spacer, found her way to one of the many messchambers.

XIII

John Albion was/is/will be living/dying/dead; sucked into the dead/dying void. John Albion had been/is/will be sitting in the warmth of her home and talking of something very small, something very alien, something very much in his bones which has/is/will be killed/killing him. Conjugate the tenses of time travel. Verbs are illusory.

A disease. An organism. The marrow. The blood. An explosion of time, but biological time; inescapable, certain. A searching. A sampling. A yearning, a leave-taking, a sudden aching absence. A movement of machines. A discovery. A synthesis. An ampule of clear fluid. A quest. A death.

Despite or because of? Too soon or too late? An idiot's question, a useless knowledge. What is/was/will be/is/was/will be. Immutable mutability; the ultimate paradox.

A discovery, a quest, an ampule in the thigh. A walk down the corridor of Azteca Sal, a seat in the midst of confusion. Because they always were/are/will be.

XIV

Noise. Fumes. Dim swirls of ersatz smoke. Raucousness. Belligerence in the corners. Shapes hulking and moving through labyrinths of sound and scent.

She sat, ignored except by the trays that brought her food and drink, accepted the flat notes she pressed upon their surfaces. She felt the small curious tensions her presence produced as though, without a halt in the uproar, she was being watched, evaluated, measured and metered on scales she only dimly comprehended. She, in turn, watched and measured.

A spacer moved by her for the fourth time. There were three others of him in the room, and each apparition ignored the other three. Another spacer, gray hair cut ragged about her gray face, leaned over a nearby table.

"When is it?" she pleaded. "When is it?" And received four conflicting answers in reply.

Music from somewhere, as disjointed as the echoes of the room. Dancing of a sort, on tables at the far side. Trays floating and bobbing among the shapes, never spilling, never knocking, ever present. And, once, a familiar face.

Seamed and gnarled, a river of scar tissue and a misplaced eye. No mistaking that, but though she raised her face to his passing and called, he did not look back. She wavered, uncertain, then pushed away from the table and crossed the room.

"Hey . . ." she began.

The hideous face turned, the eye winked.

"Yeah, sure, knocker. But I keep my nose out of my own business, see?"

She nodded, found her table again. Soon afterward she returned to her own cabin, curled on the bunk with one hand over her thigh, slept fitfully.

She spent the second day sprawled on a chair in the messchamber. Watching the eddies of the crowd, the changing sounds and moving faces, drinking sparingly. In the evening someone offered her a vial of stoneapples; she took a small sniff, returned the vial with thanks, and it disappeared back into the crowd.

The third evening someone finally approached her. A slim spacer, a woman in middle years with quick, nervous eyes and a thin mouth, two or three scars meandering down the curves of her neck.

"Share your table, knocker?" the spacer said and swung her legs over a stool, dropped her drink on the table, slouched down and peered over.

"Sure. Want another?"

"Alla time. Name's Kalya."

"Name's unimportant."

"Up to you, knocker." Kalya captured a passing tray and ordered the offered drink. "You waiting for something special?"

"Jump time."

The spacer smiled. "On which side of regs?"

"Whichever side I can find it."

"Cash?"

"Sure."

The drink arrived and was paid for, then the spacer stood from the table. "Follow me, knocker. There's always a spare coil somewhere."

XV

They followed the mazes of the station, branchings and turnings, and Kalya always ahead or beside her, words tumbling forth as she waved her drink to punctuate her sentences. Spacers called it "coiling," only knockers called it "jumping." This was one of the better Sals, always something going on. Sure, there were always illicit coils on a Sal. GalSec made sweeps for them, but all you had to do was coil forward to see when the sweep was, then move the coils to different whens; it wasn't hard, you dismantled them and put them through the coil that remained behind. Yeah, sometimes you saw a bust, no help for it: if you made it, you made it; if you didn't, you didn't. A game. No care. Small, one-person coils, some larger, some as big as an entire mess-chamber, but those were difficult to maintain; the power drain had to be managed and camouflaged from GalSec. There was one here at Azteca Sal, a party, maybe she'd like to try it, sure, it'll get you there, we'll drop you off on our way, nothing like it. You're loose, knocker, know that? And tense, like a spacer on job. You're not GalSec 'cause I'd have seen you, or you wouldn't be here, would you? Jarl tipped me, you're quick. Here, knocker. Here.

A door like any other on Sal, a gleaming metal circle with palm receiver on the right side, protruding slightly from the brushed silver gleam. Kalya pushed her palm to the plate, the door sphinctered open and they stepped forward.

Into nothingness.

She spun, seeking the door, but Kalya grasped her arm, laughing.

"Easy, knocker, easy."

She glanced down to where her feet floated, toes pointing down, nothing underfoot; a darkness from which her companion stood as the only illuminated figure on a blackened stage. "Easy, easy, easy." Her hand spread urgently along her thigh, her throat constricted, knees flexed instinctively to absorb the impact of a fall. But there were no swift rushings of air past her frightened cheeks. Kalya laughed. Shudder. Strain.

"Easy, easy. This is only the entrance, we're not into it yet. Calm, knocker. Quiet."

She straightened, touched her hip-pouch, chin, hair. Wriggled her toes experimentally against the resilient emptiness. Calmed.

"When are you headed?" Kalya asked.

"Fourteen even, two down."

"Cash?"

She fumbled at her pouch, produced a fistful of notes, handed them over.

"Good. I'll toss it into coil, we'll get you there. Ready?" The spacer hooked an arm over an invisible something and, reaching out her other arm, offered it for support.

Floating, unable to imagine the next stage, she drifted passively on Kalya's proferred arm. Felt the roundness of a door circling her. Kalya pushed them through and the invisible door snicked shut.

XVI

For we exist in time. Time is what binds molecules to make your brown eyes, your yellow hair, your thick fingers. Time changes the structures, alters hair or fingers, dims the eyes, immutably mutating reality. Time, itself unchanging, is the cosmic glue, the universal antisolvent that holds our worlds together.

Passage through a coil releases time, and the body dies. Energy remains, the components, the atoms remain but their structure is random, for the glue has been stripped away and the time-bound base no longer exists. When coiling ceases, time rebuilds the molecules to its own specifications, the glue snaps back and the self in time is recreated.

But the soul, the mind, the essence has no time, dwells in an eternity and is bound to the "now" only as it is bound within the molecules of the moment, only as it is caught in the cosmic glue. Matter, here, is transcended, the sum of the parts is more than the whole, and is capable of existence apart from the base. An analogy: mind as gas, time as the sphere in which the gas is enclosed. Break the sphere, divorce mind from time, and the essence is free to roam eternity, consistent only unto itself. Drugs release the mind from a realization of time, temporarily. Pain, starvation, flagellation, intense mysticism release the mind but, again, temporarily. By defrauding the brain, by convincing it for the hour or the day that there is no true physical base, the mind reaches toward infinite ecstasy, encompasses a portion of the god-head before it is snapped back to the temporal.

And coiling releases the mind. By destroying time, by revoking the bindings. Coiling is the possibility of endless transcendence, broken only by an act of will.

XVII

As though signaled by the shutting of the portal, bright colors, sounds, smells leaped from the room before her, random coalitions of color and shape danced by too swiftly for her mind to give them meaning, and the deafening noise battered at her ears. Chaos. Bewilderment. Fear.

Kalya laughed and stepped into the maelstrom, crying, "Come, join the party, the party, the party," and was lost to sight.

"Kalya! Wait! How?" Nothing. She strained her eyes, searching the moving seas before her for a glimpse of a familiar face, arm, anything, but the rushing refused to yield coherence. Complicated abstractions presented themselves, vanished, reformed, exploded into a million further abstractions; rationality exiled from the universe; the senses reeled.

It is a hoax, she thought bitterly. *A paltry joke played on a stupid knocker. A fraud.* And she flung herself forward.

A brief wrenching as she passed the barrier, a metaphysical twist and she was within. She glanced down, once, and screamed, closed her eyes, refused to glance at what she had become/was becoming again. Sound and color sliced through, quick hard lines that melted, honey-like, at her ears and became only slow thunders. Infinitesimal tastes hovering through the air, past and presences, a million brushings and her brain lost in sensations for which there were no names, the ordering of the universe exploded in a spacer's game.

"When are we?" she demanded of a flickering form. "Where are we? What? How?"

"It is the end of the universe," the void said seriously. "Very popular. Quite pretty. Look."

She looked and would not look again, turned and fled through the fabric of the room.

"Stay," she commands a passing face. "Help, stay!"

The face dissolves before her, and a voice says, "Why here? When did you come? How?"

"Kalya brought me, I'm lost."

"Bitch! I told her to clear, but she meddles." The sense of glare, an amorphous swirling, a purposeful stride.

"No, don't leave me!"

An impatient hand, a jerk that sends her stumbling after the form. Which changes even as she watches it, shifts through the spectrum, becomes, briefly, a quick warm scent on the air, spills outward, condenses. And still the image of a hand on the image of her arm, dragging her through chaos.

"Kalya! Bitch!"

"No," she pleads. "Just let me out, please."

"When?" the jellyfish demands.

"Fourteen even, two down. Please."

The dragging changes direction. She abandons herself to it, cuts off visual impressions, feels the insidious tickling of change. Then the sensations lessen, disappear, and she opens her eyes to find herself back in the room of nothingness, still grasped by her rescuer.

The face stabilized, somewhere between the scarred monstrosity of Nueva Azteca and the smooth youthfulness of Augustine.

"When are you?" she asked.

"Two years after Augustine. Just passing through. Stopped at the party. Didn't know."

"What happened?"

He shrugged, a quick motion of the shoulders beneath the soft scales of his robe. "Spacers get used to it, get their kicks that way. Frame of mind."

"But a ship, it's not like when . . ."

"Different. Ship coil's phased, quick. That one's not, completely random, not linked to a durator."

"So when are we now? How do I get back?"

The spacer grinned, stretching one scar wide, and reached a hand through blackness. A twisting, a writhing and she cried in fear, believing that the insane influence of the room had entered even here. But the twisting settled, the darkness remained intact. The spacer palmed open a door and ushered her into a corridor.

"Fourteen even, two down. Ship well, knocker." The spacer popped back through the door, and the snick of its closing echoed in the empty hall.

XVIII

She gazed down the pitted and pock-marked corridor, noting the stains on the stainless walls, the crackings in the floor underfoot. Wondered briefly if another trick had been played on her, if she had been deposited far in the future rather than three months in the past. Decided that she was not going to re-enter the insane party to find out and began walking down the hall, looking for a known place from which she could chart her course back to the intake port.

She peered surreptitiously at the spacers she passed but found no one familiar, even considering the time-jumping fluidity of a spacer's face. Yet, after a time, she spotted a face that looked, if not familiar, at least friendly, and she approached.

"Spacer?"

"Yeah?"

"When is it?"

The spacer stared at her, taking in all the small differences that branded her as a knocker, and smiled.

"Fourteen even, two down. Last I checked."

"Thanks. Where's the intake port?"

"Same place it always is. Follow that corridor, take a right, at the second intersect and you'll find it."

She found it. The agent irised open the window and peered out.

"Yeah?"

"I want passage on the *Claudia Frankl*, it ought to be through here tomorrow."

A swift hum of machinery. "Right, there's space. First class, second class, nothing in stasis."

"Give me first class, I don't care where."

She pressed her thumb to the plate and a bright vermilion flashed across the face of it.

"Here, knocker, gimme your thumb a minute."

She pressed her thumb against the new plate and the agent palmed it, disappeared, came back a moment later carrying her credit plate and the sack of belongings with which she had entered Azteca Sal, three months in the future.

"Arrived yesterday morning through the cargo coil. Here, look, here's the notation on the log. So I'll enter it in the PDL for, um, seventeen odd, four down, and when the agent up the line opens the PDL, there it'll be, bright and clear. And the agent'll shoot the stuff down the line, and I'll receive it yesterday and give it to you today. Enter time-change in your credit tape, right. And next time, knocker, take your gear with you, it's simpler that way. Try your thumb again."

This time bright green glowed from the panel, and she took her sack.

"Can I have a bunk for the night?"

"Sure, one in Temp'll cost you ten, plus six for cargo-jump, press again. Level A, section nine, bunk fourteen. Down the corridor, first to the right, one up. Be at Intake at fourteen two tomorrow, sharp. The shuttle doesn't wait."

"Thanks."

"Sure, knocker."

She stowed her gear in the locker at the foot of bunk 14, checked the time, then piled her clothes over the locker and swung in. Spent no time thinking of the room in which she had traveled time; her mind settled on the future, on tomorrow, and for the first time in her quest she did not sleep at all.

XIX

We'll get off at Augustine Sal, yes, and jump to somewhen where neither of us has been before. And he'll have taken the medicine, of course. A small home somewhere, a place that needs engineers so we'll be able to work. In the quiet, like the beginning, me and John, John and me, until it's time for Augustine. Since it has to happen.

He'll be changed, of course, but he'll remember me. His hands are swift and gentle, his hips are sweet. Brown and golden, brown and golden under my hands, between my thighs, laughing softly at midnight from a soft bed. When he looks toward the sky his eyes narrow against the glare, with small crinkles at the corners. Brown. His mouth is honey.

Some new star, perhaps, some just-discovered world, to build a city, a seatown, a spiraling cluster of lights and sounds. Such solid geometry we make together, me and John, John and me. New animals, new plants, we'll have a garden and he'll take a small greenery in his palms and urge it easily to the soil; things leap to life at our touch, cities and subways, fruits and flowers, tiny birds rest on his shoulders.

And to wake to find him sleeping, thighs under my knees, arm across my stomach, head on my breast, his breath is easy as he sleeps, and his hair spills over my shoulders, brown and golden, brown and golden. As it was before, and for almost forever. Until Augustine. Of course.

He'll open the door, smile, open the door, irising to his face and hands, to his legs and smile, to his chest and arms.

When he sings his voice cracks, leaves him stranded in laughter on a high, subversive note. He'll build vaulting arches across the seas, from my city to my city, and together we'll shape worlds.

Until Augustine.

Until Augustine.

XX

She stood before the closed shutter of his cabin, feeling tension twist knots upon knots within her. Pressed the call button on the wall. Pause. Pause. He's not here. He's asleep. He's not answering. He's. . .

"Yes? What is it?" Suspicious.

"Mr. Ab'naua? I have something for you."

"Who are you?"

"It's medicine."

"A medicine? Who *are* you?"

"Please, Mr. Ab'naua. John, please let me in."

The door sphinctered open suddenly and he stared at her.

It was as though he carried a fire within him, an inward light that bathed his skin with a deep bronze glow. That ate him from within, for his cheeks were deep and hollow, his eyes impossibly large in his narrow face, his wrists and ankles much too heavy for the thinness of his limbs. A medicinal smell reeked from the room behind him, crept out into the corridor as he frowned at her.

"May I come in, John?"

His eyes hardened, hand moved toward the door's controls.

"You must be mistaken. My name is Johan."

She glanced at the back of his neck, where her fingers had often massaged the tension from him. Glanced at his hand resting at his side, at the slant of his shoulders, the curve of his hips. She could have sculpted each slight plane and angle of him in plasteen, with her eyes closed, despite the ravages of the disease.

"John," she repeated positively.

"Sorry, lady, the name's Johan." His hand touched the controls, but she caught his shoulder with one hand and with the other forced his face toward her. A deliberate, furtive blankness echoed in his eyes.

No, she thought furiously. I shall not be robbed of an ending to this, I shall not be stripped of seven year's wandering. She snatched her vibraknife from the pouch at her hip and, before he could respond, she sliced through the skin of her leg, reached within and withdrew the ampule, held it red and dripping before him. He stared from it to her face, to her bleeding thigh, to the vial once again.

"It's for your marrow disease," she snapped. "It's the cure. I've been following you for seven years to give it to you and now, by damn, you're going to take it."

His hand rose, then grabbed the vial. He snatched at her arm and pulled her into the cabin.

XXI

His eyes were the wrong color. Teeth smaller and more even than she remembered them to be, lips thinner. But his broad fingers were unchanged, and she watched them expertly stitch the incision, spray a healer over the area. The deep tingling of healing tissue warmed her thigh, drove out the coolness of seven years' constant anesthesia.

Shimmering bottles lined the walls of the room. The table was littered with tubes and cans, the foot of the bunk held tiny reels of books scattered among the jars. She looked at them as she told him of the research, the synthesis, the quest. Inspected them, rather than inspect the harsh, bright, wrong light of his eyes.

He listened impatiently, fingers tapping against the cleaned ampule, and interrupted her before she had finished.

"Yes, naturally, you've come a great distance," he said, waving away her travels with a sweep of his unchanged hand. "But, of course, you didn't see those planets as I did, you couldn't know, could you? I've been so far . . ." And he told of a search for health, of one frustration after another, of failures on differing planets, of promises made and promises broken. He talked of healers and doctors and those who cure through the soul; of the resurrected natives of Gardenia and the immortal proto-organisms of Neuhafen. Expounded. Declaimed. Praised and excused. Wise men, healers, saints, gurus. Charlatans. His wrong-colored eyes glowed, his hands moved impatiently through the air as he described the promises of the healer he had changed his name to visit.

"And of course, I was suspicious when you called me 'John,'" he explained. "If GalSec knew . . . But they won't. This man, think monk on Augustine, he's spent much time on Neuhafen, he's communed with the proto-organisms. I've been there, of course, but you simply can't make any contact with them, fleetingly, like that. This man spent *decades*. And, listen, he can cure me. He . . . he can make me immortal!"

"But *this* is the cure," she told him through her confusion, and he smiled, lofted the bottle, watched it spiral through the air and made no move to catch it. She cried out, grabbed it before it shattered on the floor. Crouched, staring at him.

"But it's no good to me," he explained. "The monk can't cure me unless I'm ill, that makes sense, doesn't it? And to be immortal, to live forever! He can really do it, I've heard from people who've known people, I have it documented, here, and here. Take this one, read it, it'll convince you."

"But, John . . ." she protested, reaching the ampule toward him. He waved the vial away without looking at it.

"No, really, he can, it's all here. I know. I didn't believe it at first either, but this will change your mind, I know it will. Here, take it to your cabin with you, keep it, I have another copy."

"*John* . . ." with despair.

"Johan, please. Of course, it was quite kind of you to bring me the stuff. You couldn't tell that it would be useless, could you? I had no inkling, of course, but this thing of mine is actually a blessing, you have to consider it as a catalyst, if it weren't for that the monk wouldn't even touch me. He's a saint! A wonderful man, he'll change and cure me, they say he's immortal himself, you know, but he claims that immortality isn't important once you've reached the higher planes. We can't all do that, naturally, we have to settle for simple immortality and wait for time to mature us enough so that we can attain sainthood too. It takes time and work, I know, but I'll have forever to do it in!"

"John, you're going to die on Augustine!"

"What? Nonsense, of course not. Listen, this monk, this saint . . ."

XXII

So she decided that he wasn't John any more after all. That he was indeed Johan, someone who carried within him the essence of her lover, but transformed, transmuted, beyond her. She spent the remainder of the trip in her cabin, disembarked, pursued by angry bursar, at Augustine Sal and watched the *Claudia Frankl* shimmer from her life.

And, when you come to cases, John *had* died on Augustine. Had/is/will.

Which is paltry consolation.

She could have entered the coil at Augustine Sal and burned time away in a blaze of confusion. Could have died for love in the bleakness of space. Wandered, unconsolable, among the stars. Done any number of dramatic things. But she wasn't a very dramatic woman, so she booked passage for Terra, arrived three months after her departure. Returned to her work, raised her children and, eventually, died of old age. Was puffed to chemicals in the mortuary, with appropriate ceremony.

And that was that.

THE SEESAW

A. E. VAN VOGT

A. E. van Vogt is one of the towering figures of twentieth-century science fiction. His name itself is somehow alien and science-fictional, though it is merely of Dutch origin, and he himself a mild-mannered inhabitant of Los Angeles. For nearly forty years he has amazed and delighted readers with his fast-moving, often baffling novels—The World of Null-A, Slan, The Voyage of the Space Beagle, *and many more. For me the van Vogt works that best evoke the strangeness of the future are* The Weapons Makers *and its companion,* The Weapons Shops of Isher. *The story reprinted here is a prolog to that great series, giving us just the merest glimpse into the world of the weapons shops—but it provides a good sample of that sense of disorientation that is van Vogt's specialty, and it offers as well a deliciously cosmic insight into the perils of time travel that is an appropriate conclusion to this collection.*

MAGICIAN BELIEVED TO HAVE HYPNOTIZED CROWD

June 16, 1947— Police and newspapermen believe that Middle City will shortly be advertised as the next stopping place of a master magician. When he comes they are prepared to extend him a hearty welcome if he will condescend to explain exactly how he fooled hundreds of people into believing they saw a strange building, apparently a kind of gunshop.

The building seemed to appear on the space formerly, and still, occupied by Aunt Sally's Lunch and Patterson Tailors. Only employees were inside the two aforementioned shops, and none noticed any untoward event. A large, brightly shining sign featured the front of the gunshop, which had been so miraculously conjured out of nothingness. The sign constituted the first evidence that the entire scene was nothing but a masterly illusion. For from whatever angle one gazed at it, one seemed to be staring straight at the words, which read:

> FINE WEAPONS
> THE RIGHT TO BUY WEAPONS
> IS THE RIGHT TO BE FREE

The window display was made up of an assortment of rather curiously shaped guns, rifles as well as small arms; and a glowing sign in the window stated:

> THE FINEST ENERGY WEAPONS
> IN THE KNOWN UNIVERSE

Inspector Clayton of the Investigation Branch attempted to enter the shop, but the door seemed to be locked. A few moments later, C. J. (Chris) McAllister, reporter of the *Gazette-Bulletin*, tried the door, found that it opened, and entered.

Inspector Clayton attempted to follow him, but discovered that the door was again locked. It is believed that McAllister went through to the back, as several spectators reported seeing him. Immediately after his reappearance, the strange building vanished as abruptly as it had appeared.

Police state they are baffled as to how the master magician created so detailed an illusion for so long a period before so large a crowd. They are prepared to recommend his show, when it comes, without reservation.

[AUTHOR'S NOTE: The foregoing account did not mention that the police, dissatisfied with the affair, attempted to contact McAllister for a further interview, but were unable to locate him. Weeks have passed, and he has still not been found.]

What did happen to McAllister from the instant that he found the door of the gunshop unlocked?

There was a curious quality about the gunshop door. It was not so much that it opened at his first touch as that, when he pulled, it came away like a weightless thing. McAllister had the impression that the knob had freed itself into his palm.

He stood quite still, startled. He wondered how it was that Inspector Clayton, a minute earlier, had found the door locked. His thought was like a signal. From behind him boomed the voice of the inspector:

"Ah, McAllister, I'll handle this now."

It was dark inside the shop beyond the door, too dark to see anything, and somehow, his eyes wouldn't accustom themselves to the intense gloom. Pure reporter's instinct made him step forward toward the blackness that pressed from beyond the rectangle of door. Out of the corner of one eye, he saw Inspector Clayton's hand reaching for the door handle that his own fingers had let go a moment before. And he knew without considering it that if the police officer could prevent it, no reporter would get inside the building. His head was still turned, his gaze more on the police inspector than on the darkness in front. And it was as he began another step forward that the remarkable thing happened.

The door handle would not allow Inspector Clayton to touch it. It twisted in some queer way, in some *energy* way, for it was still there, a strange, blurred shape. The door itself, without visible movement, so swift it was, was suddenly touching McAllister's heel. Light, almost weightless, was that touch. And then, before he could think or react to what had happened, the momentum of his forward movement had carried him inside. As he breasted the darkness, there was a sudden, enormous tensing along his nerves. Then the door shut tight, the brief sensation of pain faded. Ahead was a brightly lit shop; behind were unbelievable things!

For McAllister, the moment that followed was one of blank impression. He stood, body twisted awkwardly, only vaguely conscious of the shop's interior. But he was tremendously aware in the brief moment before he was interrupted of what lay beyond the transparent panels of the door through which he had come.

There was no blackness, no Inspector Clayton, no dingy row of shops across the way. It was not even the same street. There was no street. Instead, a peaceful park spread there. Beyond it, brilliant under a noon sun, glowed a city so colossal that McAllister stared blankly. From behind him, a low, musical, woman's voice said:

"You will be wanting a gun?"

McAllister was not ready to stop gazing at the vision of a city, but he turned automatically at the sound. And because everything was still like a dream, the city scene faded almost instantly. His mind focused on the young woman who was advancing slowly from the rear section of the store. She had a slender, well-shaped body, brown eyes and neat, wavy brown hair. She was smiling pleasantly, and her simple frock and sandals seemed so normal at first glance that he gave them no further thought.

He said: "What I can't understand is why the police officer, who tried to follow me, couldn't get in. And where is he now?"

The woman's smile faded. She studied him with a faint frown. She said at last, slowly: "Naturally, a policeman couldn't get in. We know that people consider it silly of us to keep the ancient feud alive." Her voice grew firmer. "We even know how clever the propaganda is that stresses the silliness of our stand.

Meanwhile, we never allow any of *her* men in here. We continue to take our principles very seriously."

She paused as if she expected comprehension from him. But McAllister saw from the puzzlement creeping into her eyes that the expression on his face was not satisfactory to her. *Her* men! The young woman had spoken the words as if she were referring to a personage, and in direct reply to his use of the words, police officer. He meant stolid Inspector Clayton, of the Middle City force, whereas she meant—McAllister couldn't decide. What was clear was that *her* men, whoever she was, were policemen, and they weren't allowed in this gunshop. So the door was hostile, and wouldn't admit them. An emptiness grew in McAllister's mind, matching the hollowness that was beginning to afflict the pit of his stomach, a sense of unplumbed depths, the first, staggering conviction that all was not as it should be.

The girl said in a sharper tone: "You mean, you know nothing of all this, that for generations the gunmaker's guild has existed in this age of devastating energies as the common man's protection against enslavement. The right to buy guns—" She stopped again, her narrowed eyes searching him; then: "Come to think of it, there's something very illogical about you. Your outlandish clothes—you're not from the northern farm plains, are you?"

He shook his head dumbly, more annoyed with his reactions every passing second. But he couldn't help it. A tightness was growing in him, becoming more unbearable instant by instant, as if somewhere a vital mainspring were being wound to the breaking point.

The young woman went on more swiftly: "And come to think of it, it is astounding that a policeman should have tried the door, and there was no alarm."

Her hand moved. Metal flashed in it, metal as bright as steel in blinding sunlight. There was no hint of friendliness in her voice as she said: "You will stay where you are, sir, until I have called my father. In our business, with our responsibilities, we never take chances. Something is very wrong here."

Curiously, it was at that point that McAllister's mind began to function clearly. His alarm, though different, paralleled hers: How had this gunshop appeared on a 1947 street? How had he come here into this fantastic world? Something was very wrong indeed!

The girl was looking toward the wall to his left. McAllister turned, as seven miniature lights flashed on. Curious lights, a play of white and shade, a waxing and waning from one globe to the next, a rippling movement of infinitesimal increments and decrements, an incredibly delicate effect of instantaneous reaction to some super-sensitive barometer.... As the lights momentarily steadied, his gaze reverted to the girl. To his surprise, she was putting away her gun.

"The automatics are on you now," she said. She went on in a puzzled tone, "You may not realize it, but you have already upset our establishment. The lights of the automatics should have gone on the moment father pressed the buttons. They didn't. That's unnatural." She paused, frowning.

There was a chair to McAllister's right. He started for it. "Look," he began, "I don't know what you're talking about. I don't even know how I came to be in this shop."

His voice trailed. He had been half-lowered into the chair, but now he came erect. His eyes stared at lettering that shone above a glass case of guns behind her. He said hoarsely: "Is that—a calendar?"

She followed his gaze. "Yes, it's June third. What's wrong?"

That was wrong in itself. This was June sixteenth, not June third. But that wasn't what he meant.

"I mean—" McAllister caught himself with an effort. "I mean those figures above that. I mean—what year is this?"

The young woman looked surprised. She started to say something, then stopped and backed away.

"Don't look like that," she said. "This is the 4784th year of the Imperial House of Isher. It's quite all right."

McAllister finished sitting down. Not even surprise came to his aid. The events were beginning to fall into a kind of distorted pattern. The building front superimposed on those two 1947 shops, the way the door had acted, the great exterior sign with its odd linking of freedom and the right to buy weapons, the actual display of weapons in the window, the finest energy weapons in the known universe! . . . He grew aware that the girl was talking earnestly with a tall, gray-haired man who was standing on the threshold of the door through which she had originally come.

There was a tenseness in the way they were standing. Their low-spoken words made a blur of sound in his ears, strange and unsettling. McAllister could not quite analyze the meaning of it until the girl turned, and said, "What is your name?"

McAllister gave it.

The girl hesitated, then: "Mr. McAllister, my father wants to know what year you're from!"

The gray-haired man stepped forward. "I'm afraid," he said gravely, "that there is no time to explain. What has happened is that for which we have constantly had to be on the alert: that once again would come one who lusted for unlimited power; and who, to attain tyranny, must necessarily seek first to destroy us. Your presence here is a manifestation of the energy force that she has turned against us—something so new that we did not even suspect it was being used against us. But I have no time to waste. Get all the information you can, Lystra, and warn him of his own personal danger." The man turned. The door closed noiselessly behind his tall figure.

McAllister asked, "What did he mean—personal danger?"

He saw that girl's brown eyes were uneasy as they watched him. "It's hard to explain," she said in an uncomfortable voice. "That building over there is the source of the energy."

His alarm was gone. The gray-haired man seemed to know what it was all about. That meant there should be no difficulty getting home again. As for all this danger to the gun-makers' guild, that was their worry, not his.

The window occupied a space beside the "automatics," and the strange thing about it was that McAllister didn't remember having seen it earlier. He gazed for a moment at the massive, streamlined building, and then turned to ask the girl about the window. She cringed away from his movement, and said shakily: "Don't think I'm being silly, and don't be offended—but for your life's sake don't go near anybody!"

McAllister drew back. "Now, look," he began. "I want to get this clear. We're in no danger, providing I don't touch you, or come near you. Is that right?"

She nodded. "The floor, the walls, every piece of furniture, in fact the entire shop is made of non-conducting material."

McAllister had a sense of being balanced on a tightrope over a bottomless abyss. This girl had a way of implying danger without making clear what the danger was. He forced calm into his mind.

"Let's start," he said, "at the beginning. How did you and your father know that I was not of" —he paused before the odd phrase, then went on— "of this time?"

"Father X-rayed you," the girl said. "He X-rayed the contents of your pockets. That was how he first found out what was the matter. You see, the X-rays themselves became carriers of the energy with which you're charged. That's what was the matter. That's why the automatics wouldn't focus on you, and—"

"Energy—charged?" said McAllister.

The girl was staring at him. "Don't you understand?" she gasped. "You've come across seven thousand years of time. And of all the energies in the universe, time is the most potent. You're charged with trillions of trillions of time-energy units. If you should step outside this shop, you'd blow up Imperial City and half a hundred miles of land beyond."

"You—" It was her father's voice, coming from behind them— "you, sir, could conceivably destroy the earth.... The danger is so great, the importance of getting you back where you came from so urgent, that I have already called the Weapon Makers' Council and—"

He paused. "Ah, gentlemen," he said.

He spoke past McAllister, who turned with a start. Men were

coming out of the solid wall, where the window had been, lightly, easily, as if it were a door, and they were stepping across the threshold . . . one, two, three . . . thirty. They were stern-faced men, all except one. That one glanced at McAllister, then stopped with a half-amused smile.

He said quietly: "How else do you think we could have survived all these years if we hadn't been able to transmit objects over distance? The Isher soldiery have always been eager to block our sources of supply. Incidentally, my name is Cadron—Peter Cadron."

Before McAllister could reply, a heavy-faced individual said, "My name is Dresley." He faced about immediately, and began, "We have gathered here because it is obvious that the source of the new energy is the great building just outside this shop."

He motioned towards the magic wall, which, McAllister saw, was again a window. This time, however, the window could not distract him, and now he saw that neither near that building nor in the park was a living person visible. Everywhere was evidence of man's dynamic labor, but no men and no movement. Even the trees stood motionless in that breathless, sunlit day.

A hand, reaching from behind him, gingerly held out a limp, grayish thing. McAllister stared at it, as the young man walked around in front of him, and said: "This is an insulated suit, and it is our hope and yours. What we have in mind is an application of a sort of an energy and fulcrum principle. You are to be the weight at the long end of a kind of energy 'crowbar,' which lifts the greater weight at the short end. You will go back seven thousand years in time. The machine and all of that building, to which your body will be tuned, will move ahead in time on a basis of comparative weights, only a few seconds, but enough to break all the matter tensions of the space it occupies. It will become useless to the Imperial forces and no longer a danger to us."

"In that way," said another man, "we shall gain the time we need to counteract the entire attack."

McAllister accepted the suit, and stood holding it in his

hands. He looked from it to the man, recalling vaguely that he had heard about such things before, in a different application.

"I get it," he remembered suddenly, aloud. "The lever principle, the old idea that if you had a lever long enough, and a suitable fulcrum, you could move the earth out of its orbit."

"Exactly." It was Dresley, the heavy-faced individual. "Only this lever works in time, and you at the long end have to swing seven thousand years."

Still McAllister hesitated. The room seemed insufferably hot. Perspiration streaked down his cheeks, and he felt sick with uncertainty. His gaze fell on the girl, standing silent and subdued near the front door. He strode toward her, and either his glare or his presence was frightening, for she turned white.

"Look," he said. "I'm in this as deep as hell. What's the risk of this thing? I've got to feel that I have some chance. These fellows are too smooth. Tell me, what's the catch?"

The girl was gray now, almost as gray and dead-looking as the suit the young man was holding. "It's the friction," she mumbled finally. "You may not get all the way back to 1947. You see, you'll be a sort of dead weight and—"

McAllister whirled away from her. He climbed into the soft, almost flimsy suit, crowding the overall-like shape over his neatly pressed clothes. "It comes tight over the head, doesn't it?" he asked.

"Yes." It was Lystra's father who answered. "As soon as you pull that zipper shut, the suit will become completely invisible. To outsiders, it will seem as if you have on only your ordinary clothes. The suit is fully equipped. You could live on the moon inside it."

"What I don't get," complained McAllister, "is why I have to wear it. I got here all right without it."

He frowned. "Just a minute. What becomes of the energy with which I'm charged, when I'm bottled up in this insulation?"

He saw by the stiffening expressions of those around him that he had touched on a vast subject.

"So that's it!" he snapped. "The insulation is to prevent me from losing any of that energy. That's how it can make a 'weight.' I have no doubt there is a connection from this suit to that other machine. Well, it's not too late."

He was tugging at the zipper, when four men grabbed him. Strong fingers locked the zipper tight; and he was being carried irresistibly towards the door when the voice of Peter Cadron snapped a command.

The forward movement slowed, then petered out. McAllister grew blurrily aware of Cadron, his head held proudly erect.

Cadron said quietly: "Gentlemen, I know that every minute counts, but this unseemly haste is degrading. At this point, therefore, we rise above our fears, and we say to this unhappy young man: 'Have courage. We can guarantee nothing, we cannot even state exactly what will happen to you. But we say, if it lies in our power to help you, that help you shall have.' And now—we must protect you from the devastating psychological pressures that would otherwise destroy you, simply but effectively."

Too late, McAllister noticed that the others had turned their faces away from that extraordinary wall—the wall that had already displayed so vast a versatility. He did not even see who pressed the activating button for what followed.

There was a flash of dazzling light. For an instant he felt as if his mind had been laid bare; and against that nakedness the voice of Peter Cadron pressed like some ineradicable engraving stamp: "To retain your self-control and your sanity—this is your hope; this you will do in spite of everything! And, for your own sake, speak of your experience only to scientists or to those in authority whom you feel will understand and help. Good luck!"

So strong remained the effect of that brief flaring light that he felt only vaguely the touch of their hands on him, propelling him.

He felt himself falling.

He landed on his outstretched hands, and saw presently that

he was lying on a sidewalk. He climbed to his feet. A pall of curious faces gawked at him; and there was no park, no great city. Instead, a bleak row of one-story shops made a dull pattern on either side of the street.

A man's voice floated towards him out of a blur of other sounds: "I'm sure it's the reporter who went into that weapon shop."

So he was back in his own time. The same day. He moved off, as the man's penetrating voice spoke again: "He looks kind of sick to me. I wonder what—"

He heard no more. But he thought, "Sick!" These people would never understand how sick. But somewhere on Earth must be a scientist who could help him. The record was that he hadn't exploded.

He was walking rapidly now, and clear of the crowd. Once, he looked back, and saw that the people were dispersing in the aimless fashion of folks who had lost their center of interest. McAllister turned a corner, and forgot them.

"I've got to decide."

The words were loud, close. It took a moment to realize that he had spoken them.

Decide? He hadn't thought of his position as requiring a decision. Here he was. Find a scientist. . . . If that was a decision, he had already made it. The question was, whom? Memory came of his old physics professor at City College. Automatically, he turned into a phone booth and fumbled for a nickel. With a sickening sense of disaster, he remembered that he was dressed in an all-enclosing transparent suit, and that his money was inside. He drew back, and stopped, shaken. What was *happening*?

It was night, in a brilliant, glowing city. He was standing on the boulevard of an avenue that stretched jewel-like into remote distance. A street that flamed with a soft light that gleamed up from its surface. A road of light, like a river flowing under a sun that shone nowhere else, straight and smooth.

He walked along for uncomprehending minutes, fighting a

wild hope, but at last the thought forced through to his consciousness. Was this again the age of Isher and the gunmakers? It could be. It looked right, and it meant they had brought him back. After all, they were not evil, and they would save him if they could. For all he knew, weeks had passed in *their* time.

He began to hurry. Find a weapon shop. A man walked by him, and McAllister turned and called after him. The man paused curiously, and looked back, then continued on his way. McAllister had a brief picture of dark, intense eyes, and a visualization of a person on his way to a marvelous home of the future. It was that that made him suppress his impulse to run after the man.

He should have. It was the last person he saw on all those quiet, deserted streets. It must have been the in-between hour before the false dawn. But it was not the absence of human life that disturbed him. It was the fact that not once did he see a weapon shop.

In spite of that, his hope mounted. Soon it would be morning. Men would come out of these strange, glowing homes. Great scientists of an age of wizard scientists would examine him, not in a frenzy of haste, with the fear of destruction hanging over their minds. But quietly, in the sanity of super-laboratories.

The thought ended. He felt the *change*.

He was in the center of a blinding snow storm. He staggered from the first mighty, unexpected blow of that untamed wind. Then, bracing himself, fought for mental and physical calm.

The shining, wondrous night city was gone. Gone, too, the glowing road. Both vanished, transformed into this deadly, wilderness world. He peered through the driving snow. It was daylight, and he could make out the dim shadows of trees that reared up through the white mist of blizzard less than fifty feet away.

Instinctively, he pressed toward their shelter, and stood finally out of that blowing, pressing wind. He thought: "One minute in the distant future; the next—where?"

There was certainly no city. Only trees, an uninhabited

forest, and a bitter, primeval winter. How long he stood there, while those winds blew, and that storm raged, he had no idea. He had time for a thousand thoughts, time to realize that the suit protected him from the cold as if there were no cold; and then—

The blizzard was gone. And the trees. He stood on a sandy beach. Before him stretched a blue, sunlit sea that rippled over broken, white buildings. All around, scattered far into that shallow, lovely sea, far up into the weed-grown hills, were the remnants of a once tremendous city. Over all clung an aura of incredible age; and the silence of the long-dead was broken only by the gentle, timeless lapping of the waves.

Again came that instantaneous change. More prepared this time, he nevertheless sank twice under the surface of the vast, swift river that carried him on and on. It was hard swimming, but the insulated suit was buoyant with the air it manufactured each passing second. And, after a moment, he began to struggle purposely towards the tree-lined shore a hundred feet to his right. A thought came, and he stopped swimming. "What's the use!" The truth was as simple as it was terrible. He was being shunted from the past to the future. He was the "weight" on the long end of an energy seesaw; and in some way he was slipping farther ahead and further back each time. Only that could explain the catastrophic changes he had already witnessed. In an hour would come another change.

It came. He was lying face downward on green grass. When he looked up, he saw a half-dozen low-built buildings on the horizon of grass. They looked alien, unhuman. But his curiosity was not about them. A thought had come: How long, actually, did he remain in one particular time?

He kept an eye on his watch; and the time was two hours and forty minutes. That was his last curiosity. Period after period, as the seesaw jerked on, he remained in his one position, water or land, it made no difference to him. He did not fight it. He neither walked nor ran nor swam or even sat up. . . . Past—future—past—future—

His mind was turned inward. He had a vague feeling that

there was something he ought to do, inside his skin, not outside. Something about a decision that he had believed he must make. Funny, he couldn't recall what it was.

Beyond doubt, the gunmakers had won their respite. For at the far end of this dizzy teeter-totter was the machine that had been used by the Isher soldiers as an activating force. It too teetered past, then future, in this mad seesaw.

But that decision. He'd really have to try to think about it.

McAllister had forgotten about the personal decision he intended to make. It was so hard to think in this darkness. He opened his tired eyes, and saw that he was poised moveless in black space. There was no earth under him. He was in a time where earth did not yet exist. The darkness seemed to be waiting for some colossal event.

Waiting for him.

He had a sudden flash of understanding of what was going to happen. Wonder came then and a realization of what his decision must be . . . resignation to death!

It was a strangely easy decision to make. He was so weary. Bitter-sweet remembrance came of the day in far-gone time and space, in forgotten Italy, when he had lain half-dead on a meaningless battlefield, resigned to personal oblivion. Then he had thought that he must die so that others might live. The feeling now was the same, but stronger and on a much higher level.

How it would be worked he had no idea. But the seesaw would end in the very remote past, with the release of the stupendous temporal energy he had been accumulating with each of those monstrous swings.

He would not witness but he would aid in the formation of the planets.